CW01271550

Sh

Seventy

A.N.D. Haksar is a well-known translator of Sanskrit classics. Educated at the universities of Allahabad and Oxford, he spent many years as a career diplomat, serving as India's High Commissioner to Kenya and the Seychelles, minister to the United States and Ambassador to Portugal and Yugoslavia. His translations from the Sanskrit include the plays of Bhasa, the romance *Daśa Kumāra Charitam* of Dandin, the story collections *Hitopadeśa*, *Simhāsana Dvātrimśikā* and *Jātakamālā*, the verse anthology *Subhāshitāvali* and the first ever renditions of *Mādhavānala Katha* and *Samaya Mātrikā*, published respectively as *Madhav & Kama* and *The Courtesan's Keeper*. He has also compiled *Glimpses of Sanskrit Literature* and *A Treasury of Sanskrit Poetry* for the Indian Council for Cultural Relations.

Written in simple, unembellished language, these ribald tales of sexual intrigue, cunning and credulity provide an entertaining social documentation of how men and women lived and loved in ancient India.

—The Telegraph

Once one has read through this collection of tales, one cannot help but be – you guessed it – delighted by the earthiness of this 15th century text.

—The Asian Age

Sheherazade was a novice compared to this parrot. Its stories are bawdy, perceptive, robust, witty and utterly irresistible.

—Sunday Observe

Haksar's translation is racy and colloquial to match the simple and direct language of the original Sanskrit.

—Indian Review of Books

Some of the stories in this collection are bawdy, some are folksy, but each one of them shows a deep understanding of human nature.

—The Pioneer

Shuka Saptati
Seventy Tales of the Parrot

Translated from the Sanskrit by
A.N.D. Haksar

RUPA

Published by
Rupa Publications India Pvt. Ltd 2009
7/16, Ansari Road, Daryaganj
New Delhi 110002

Sales centres:
Allahabad Bengaluru Chennai
Hyderabad Jaipur Kathmandu
Kolkata Mumbai

ISBN: 978-81-291-1516-4

Second impression 2016

10 9 8 7 6 5 4 3 2

Typeset by Mindways Design, New Delhi

P.M.S.

For my sisters
Kiran Dhar
and
Rashmi Haksar
with love

Contents

A Note to the New Edition

The *katha* literature of Sanskrit is a treasure trove of wonderful stories of all kinds. Many, if not most, still await appropriate translation to bring them out of academic archives before today's interested readership. Such exposure would also help to make better known the often neglected aspect of Sanskrit as popular literature whose reach went beyond feudal and clerical elites to a more general public. The present work will I hope open doors to others in this direction. My thanks to Rupa & Co for bringing out this new edition. Acknowledgement is also due to Sanjana Roy Choudhury for the initial response and to Pushpanjali Borooah for her cooperation in editing the proofs and arranging a new cover. I have taken the opportunity to make a few corrections and add some more notes, mainly about the sources of verses which embellish the prose text.

Noida   A.N.D.H.
5 October 2008

Introduction

The *Shuka Saptati* is a part of the *kathá* literature of classical Sanskrit. This comprises a variety of stories, fables and narratives, sometimes in verse, but often in prose interspersed with gnomic stanzas. It is composed in relatively simple and direct language, in contrast to the more cultivated and refined styles which characterise classical *kávya* literature. The latter, which includes the poetry and plays of Kalidasa, the prose of Bána, and the works of other celebrated writers, was written essentially for cultured and sophisticated audiences. The *kathá* works catered to a wider cross-section. Best known today through the fables of the *Panchatantra* and the *Hitopadeśa*, they also include romances, adventures and fantasies whose popularity and currency over the centuries is attested to by numerous recensions and adaptations into other Indian languages.

The *Shuka Saptati* stands out among *kathá* works not so much for its unusual themes of adultery and skulduggery, as for the earthiness with which they are treated in its tales. There are few circumlocutions or polite allusions in its references to sexual and other transgressions, and the language is often blunt, sometimes to the point of crude humour. This may have shocked the pioneering historians of Sanskrit literature. Winternitz,[1] who acknowledged the *Shuka Saptati* as one of 'the most famous and popular narrative works of India', warned that its contents 'often verge to pornographical stories and some of them are outright obscene'. Keith[2] observed that the 'tales are hardly edifying; about half of them deal with breaches of the marriage bond while the rest exhibit other instances of cunning.' Indian scholars were more defensive in their comments. 'However disreputable some of the stories may be,' noted Dasgupta,[3] 'they are certainly smart and generally amusing.' Krishnamachariar[4] described them as 'stories of erotic nature, but of ultimate didactic import.'

More recent authorities in India and abroad have categorised the work simply as 'a collection of satiric mischievous wives' tales',[5] or a 'lively cycle of attractive stories'.[6] Readers at the turn of the millennium may find all these descriptions excessive, and the tales comparatively commonplace; but the work remains a good example of the picaresque narrative in Sanskrit, a language which is now associated mainly with religious, philosophic or epic literature.

♦

The structure of the *Shuka Saptati* is the traditional one of tales within tales. The frame story describes the wayward son of a merchant, who is converted to virtuous conduct by the wise talk of a parrot presented to him by his father. He then proceeds on a journey and entrusts the bird to his young wife's care. She first pines for her husband, but is soon persuaded by friends to console herself with a lover. As she sets out for the rendezvous, the clever parrot endorses her intent provided she is as smart as the woman Lakshmi in extricating herself from any ensuing problems. The lady's curiosity is aroused, and she stays at home, listening all night to the parrot's tale about Lakshmi. This pattern is repeated for sixty-nine evenings, during which the bird continues to distract the heroine from going to meet a lover with tales of cunning escapes out of complicated situations. At the end of this period she is reunited with her husband, her virtue intact, while the parrot, or *shuka*, edifies both with the last of its seventy or *saptati* tales, which emphasises the importance of forgiveness in marital concord.

Including the frame and an introductory story, there are altogether seventy-two tales in the *Shuka Saptati*. Some form a sequence of their own within the overall framework, for example, five tales about the riddle of the laughing fish (5 to 9), three about the tiger slayer (42 to 44), and two about the terrified ghost (46 and 47). Most are short by present-day standards, but some are longer than the others, like the tale of Govinda and the poison maiden (4), Rambhika and her reluctant lover (11), and the queen and the court poet of King Vikramaditya (57). Such stories are generally well rounded and include a number of homilies and aphorisms in verse. Tale 57 also contains a good example of *samasyápúrti*, the once popular practice of composing separate stanzas around a given maxim or refrain.

The rhythm of the longer stories is varied by shorter ones, such as those recounting the adventures of the intelligent Jayashri (52), the passionate Tejika (61), and Rukmini (59), who combined both qualities; and by others which are no more than brief anecdotes of ready wit, like those about the mustard thief (18), the ploughman (37), and the brahmin's sari (34). Some others of this type, for example, tales 49, 63 and 68, are obscure and obviously incomplete in the form in which they have come down. Some otherwise well-formed tales, like 60 and 64, end abruptly, probably for the same reason. The cycle also includes animal fables like the well-known 31 and 67, and some stories containing fine descriptions in the *kávya* style of the summer (23), the spring (41), and the rains (57).

Winternitz[7] considered that several Indian stories gained currency in world literature through works like the *Shuka Saptati*. He gave the example of tale 15 about the manipulated judgement, which appeared in Europe in Strassburg's *Tristan and Isolde*, and traced the motif to earlier Buddhist *játakas*. Such instances point to the existence of numerous floating stories which have periodically found their way into various *kathá* compilations in India. Many *Shuka Saptati* stories can themselves be traced to other sources like the *Kathásaritságara* and the collections of fables already mentioned. A contemporary scholar[8] has suggested that some of them are derived from the narrative work *Nanda Prabodhana* or *Upákhyana*, which centres around the kings of that name who immediately preceded the Mauryan empire in the fourth century BC, and which also features the story of the laughing fish.

Equally interesting are the sources of the over three hundred stanzas in Sanskrit and Prakrit which occur in many *Shuka Saptati* tales. The researches of Sternbach[9] showed that they include quotations from the epics and various *puránas*, the *Panchatantra* and the *Hitopadeśa*, the Chanakya and Bhartrihari anthologies, and also from well-known *kávya* works like the *Kumárasambhava* of Kalidasa, the *Mricchakatika* of Śudraka, and the *Mudrárákshasa* of Viśákhadatta. Several quotations were later interpolations, for instance those from the *Kama Sutra* in tale 57 classifying lovers and beds. Two sources, the *Mahabharata* and the *Kirátárjuniya* of Bháravi, are identified in the text; the origin of some well-known stanzas has been indicated in the end notes. The sourcing and cross referencing of *kathá* stories and verses remains a fruitful field for further research.

♦

The oldest known manuscript of the *Shuka Saptati* is from the fifteenth century AD. Academic opinion holds that the work was in existence long before it emerged in the form in which it is now available.[10] One scholar[11] traced it to the sixth century AD. Another[12] suggested that it is referred to in the eleventh century treatise on poetics, the *Shringáraprakásha* of Bhoja. More certain is its mention in Hemachandra's commentary on the *Yogashástra*, which was written after AD 1160. The *Shuka Saptati* is further known to have been adapted into Persian in AD 1329. Current scholarship dates it, as such, to not later than the second part of the twelfth century AD, though many of its stories may be much older.

The work is presently extant in two Sanskrit recensions. Their critical editions were prepared by the German scholar Richard Schmidt just over a hundred years ago, and termed by him as the *simplicior* and the *ornatior* texts. The first is attributed to a Shvetambara Jaina monk, and the second to the brahmin Chintamani Bhatta. Some scholars consider that the *simplicior* is probably older than the *ornatior*. It has a simple, sometimes abrupt style, with brief sentences and occasional condensation of the narrative to the point of obscurity. The *ornatior* is more elaborate and ornate. Both recensions contain over fifty common stories, but have differences in wording, names of some characters and verse quotations. Neither is considered the ur-text. An eastern Rajasthani version of the *Shuka Saptati* has been recorded as derived from another Sanskrit recension by Devadatta, son of Purushottama Deva.

Translations of the work have a long history. The fourteenth century adaptation of the Sanskrit text into Persian has already been mentioned. This was the *Tuti Namah* of Ziya al-din Nakhshabi, which was abridged by Muhammad Qadiri in the seventeenth century under the same name, but confined to only thirty-five stories. The Nakhshabi version was also rendered into Turkish with the omission of some bawdy tales. A translation into German from the Persian in 1822 brought the work to the West. In India, versions exist in Hindi, Kannada, Marathi, eastern Rajasthani, Telugu and Urdu. Others have been recorded in Malay, Mongolian and Newari. There is a later imitation in Sanskrit, entitled *Dinálápaniká Shuka Saptati* or *The Seventy Tales of the Parrot in Daily Conversation*. Translations into European languages exist in French, Greek, Hungarian, Polish and Russian, apart from several in German.

Qadiri's *Tuti Namah* was translated from Persian into English by F. Gladwin at the end of the last century. B. Hale Wortham's rendition of a selection of Shuka Saptati tales appeared in 1911 with the title *The Enchanted Parrot*. An examination of available records suggests that the present is the first translation of the complete work into English from the original Sanskrit.

The present translation is intended to make this ancient cycle of stories available to today's readership in modern English. It has been prepared from the Sanskrit text published by the Chowkhamba Sanskrit Serise Office of Varanasi in 1966. That text is of the *simplicior* recension, though this detail has not been mentioned in its published version. It was brought out with commentaries in Sanskrit and Hindi by Pandit Ramakanta Tripathi, which the present translator has consulted with profit but not always followed.

Apart from the invocation, the stanzas interspersing the prose text of the *Shuka Saptati* are of three kinds: narrative, descriptive and gnomic. The first type have generally been rendered in prose to maintain continuity with the overall narrative of the stories. The others have been presented in verse form for closer correspondence with the original text. The translation of both the prose and the verse portions endeavours to combine fidelity to the text with requirements of the English idiom, and some explanatory language for esoteric words like *vishakanyá*. It also attempts to convey something of the flavour of the original, which may account for the occasional use of archaisms, specially in the prose renderings. Some repetitious phrases, like those which conclude most stories, have occasionally been recast to provide variety. Each story has also been given a title for ready reference.

In the transliteration of names, those which are still current have been spelt in keeping with modern usage, for example 'Madan Vinod', and not 'Madana Vinoda'. Others have been treated in accordance with academic practice, except that diacritics have been used only to indicate long vowels.

◆

To translate the *Shuka Saptati* was a fascinating experience. The language is simple and unembellished, but the best stories are notable for their human insight and earthy humour, succinctness of presentation and suddenness of impact. Their cynical depiction of human propensities gives them a universal dimension despite the unacceptability of the attitude towards women projected in some stories. Set in scenes varying from royal courts to market places, and urban centres to village communities, they also provide an absorbing social documentation of ancient Indian conditions.

I am grateful to Renuka Chatterjee, Editor-in-Chief of HarperCollins Publishers India, for her ready response which encouraged me to undertake this translation. I would also like to thank Arpita Das for helping to edit the copy for publication and Oroon Das for designing the cover. Special appreciation is due to my son Vikram and his wife Annika for their computer assistance at a crucial juncture. Above all, I thank my wife Priti for her careful review as always of my drafts, and for her unstinting support in this as in all my endeavours.

Washington DC   A.N.D.H
August 1999

Prologue

The goddess Sháradá[1] I salute,
she of wisdom absolute,
and here narrate, so you may find
some diversion for the mind,
how a parrot's goodly sense
brought about a deliverance.

There is a city called Chandrapur which was once ruled by King Vikram Sen. At that time there lived in the city a merchant named Hari Datta and his wife Shringára Sundari. They had a son, Madan Vinod, who was married to the daughter of Som Datta, another merchant. Her name was Prabhávati.

Madan Vinod was not a good son. He did not listen to his father's advice, and was given excessively to the pursuit of pleasure. His great addictions included gambling and hunting, drinking and whoring. Seeing the bad ways of their son made Hari Datta and his wife extremely unhappy.

Hari Datta had a close friend, a brahmin named Trivikram. Observing his colleague suffer on account of his offspring, the brahmin took a worldly-wise parrot from his own home together with a mynah bird, and went to the merchant's house. 'Comrade Hari Datta,' he said, 'look after this parrot and its mate as if they were your own children. This will drive your sorrows away.'

The merchant took the parrot and gave it to his son. Madan Vinod placed the bird in a golden cage in his bedroom, and began to look after it. Once, when they were alone, the parrot addressed Madan: 'Friend,

> Because of you, your parents grieve,
> shed tears of sorrow on the ground.
> This sin, my child, will cause your fall,
> as Dev Sharma had earlier found.'

'How did that happen?' asked Madan. The parrot narrated:

The Tale of Dev Sharma

There is a town called Panchapur. A brahmin named Satya Sharma lived there with his wife Dharmasheela and a son, Dev Sharma. After completing his education, this boy went away secretly to another country without telling his father, and began to practise austerities on the banks of the river Ganga.

Once, while the young ascetic was sitting by the riverside, telling his beads, a stork flying overhead happened to shit upon

him. As he looked up, his eyes blazing with anger, the bird
was incinerated in the fire of his wrathful gaze and fell dead
to the ground.

Some time later Dev Sharma went to the house of the
brahmin Narayan to beg for alms. The brahmin's wife was at
that time busy attending to her husband. When the ascetic
expressed his displeasure at having to wait, she upbraided him
in turn. 'I am not a stork to become the victim of your anger,'
she told the murderer of that innocent bird. He, on his part,
was both amazed and scared to find that she knew about his
guilty secret. He asked her how she had come to know of this
and was despatched by her to the city of Varanasi to seek an
answer from Dharma Vyádha, the righteous butcher.[2]

In Varanasi Dev Sharma saw the butcher, vending meat and
looking like the god of death, his hands covered with blood.
He stood at a distance till the butcher took him home with
some welcoming words, and gave him something to eat after
he had first served food devotedly to his own parents.

Dev Sharma asked the butcher what made men wise. 'How
did that good woman know,' he asked, 'and how do you?' The
butcher told him:

> One who does his duties well
> as laid down in his clan traditions,
> turns his back on all distractions,
> the good, the bad, the average kind,
> and his parents always serves:

that person is the true householder,
sage and virtuous, a pious yogi,
though he be but a common man.

'She and I have become wise in this way,' the butcher added.
'And you, who go about after having abandoned your parents,
are not even worth talking to by people like me. But I do so,
considering that you are a guest.'

The brahmin then respectfully asked other questions, to
which the butcher replied:

The people who do not accord
honour and respect to those it is due
are disparaged in this world,
and after death go not to heaven.

Enlightened thus by the butcher, Dev Sharma returned to
his home, earning fame among people and a good reputation
which lived on after his death.

The Parrot and the Merchant's Wife

'You must therefore bear in mind the duties of merchants
which spring from your own family traditions,' the parrot said,
'and be respectful and attentive to your parents.'

Thus admonished, Madan went to his parents and paid them
homage. After taking their permission and consulting his wife
he then boarded a ship and went away to another country.

Madan's wife Prabhávati remained dejected for some days
after his departure. But then, tutored by some women friends

of questionable character, she became desirous of acquiring a paramour. For they would say to her:

> Man has parents and relatives
> only while he lives;
> when he dies and they come to know it,
> their love subsides that very moment.

'As you cannot have your own husband,' they urged her, 'and your body will stay young only for a short while, enjoy the fruit of your youth in love with another man.'

Persuaded by such words, Prabhávati dressed up one day for a rendezvous with another man named Guna Chandra. As she was leaving, the mynah chided her and told her not to go. She tried to kill the bird by wringing its neck, but it flew away quickly. For a moment she stood still, praying in her heart to her favourite god. Making up her mind, she then put a betel leaf in her mouth and was about to step out, when the parrot spoke up. 'May all be well with you,' it said, 'but where are you going?'

Considering the parrot's words to be an omen, the merchant's wife replied with a laugh, 'O king of parrots, I am on my way to find out what it is like to have another man for a lover.'

'That is fine, and merits doing,' said the parrot. 'But it is not easy for women of good families. Moreover it is considered disreputable. Go if you have the wits to handle any problems which may arise. Otherwise you will be in for trouble. For,

> The wicked merely watch the fun
> when problems arise.
> Like the starving lady did
> as another pulled the merchant's hair.'

The merchant's wife and her rakish friends were taken aback. 'What do you mean, parrot?' Prabhávati asked respectfully. 'Go to your lover, my beauty,' the bird replied. 'Afterwards you can listen to this long story if your pretty eyes are still interested.'

The parrot's words filled her with curiosity, and she stayed back at home. The bird then told her a story.

Seventy Tales of the Parrot

1

Lakshmi and the Unexpected Lover

In the city of Chandrávati, which was ruled by King Bhima, there lived a merchant named Mohan. His son Sudhan wished to sleep with Lakshmi, the wife of another citizen called Hari Datta; however the lady had not acquiesced till then. Once, when Hari Datta had gone out of the city, Sudhan sent to his house a professional go-between woman named Purna, who had been starving for a month without work. He paid her handsomely and she was able to so propitiate Lakshmi with words of flattery that the latter agreed to do whatever the go-between requested. 'Take the man I recommend as your lover,' Purna told her.

'This is not proper for women from good families,' Lakshmi replied, 'but I will do what I have promised you. As it is said,

> Loss of life may come to pass,
> loss of freedom, loss of wealth:
> the good will always keep their word,
> whatever else will be, will be.

Chains of iron there may be,
or curbs and nooses various,
but even stronger for the good
is their word, their bond.

Shiva endures the cosmic poison,
Kúrma the earth upon his back,
Ocean the fierce submarine fire,[1]
even today: the good will do
whatever they undertake.'

Purna was overjoyed by these words. 'Let it be just so,' she
said and, after preparing Lakshmi for love's feast, took her in
the evening to her own home. But Sudhan, the prospective
lover, was preoccupied with some other work, and failed to
appear at the appointed hour.

Lakshmi had meanwhile been aroused. 'Bring me some
other man,' she demanded, whereupon Purna was foolish
enough to bring the lady's own husband for the tryst.

'Well, what should she do when her own husband turns
up?' the parrot concluded. 'How should she go home? You or
your friends should now explain this.'

'We do not know!' Prabhávati cried. 'You must tell us!'

'Well, I will tell you if you do not go out,' said the parrot,
and she agreed not to go.

'Realising that the new arrival was her own husband,'
the parrot then said, 'she caught hold of him by his hair and,
shouting "You rogue! You always made out before me that there

is no other woman in your life apart from myself. Now I have tested you and I know!" she got very angry indeed with him. Eventually Hari Datta was able to take her home only with great difficulty and many endearments.'

Astonished and intimidated by the parrot's story, Prabhávati did not go out that night, but slept instead at home together with her band of wantons.

Here ends the first tale of Shuka Saptati

2

Yasho Devi Entices the Princess

O n the second day the merchant's wife set out as before with her friends at nightfall. On being asked, the parrot told her: 'Go where you please, my lady of the lovely hips, but only if you know what to do when there is a problem in performing a difficult deed, as did Yasho Devi.'

'Who was Yasho Devi?' Prabhávati asked. 'What was her problem? How did it happen, and what did she do?'

'If I start telling you,' said the parrot, 'it will interfere with your lovemaking. You will get angry, and that may be the end of my life.'

'Well, one should hear out what well-wishers have to say,' she replied, 'no matter if it is good or even bad.' And, with this permission, the parrot related a story.

There is a city called Nandan. Its king was also named Nandan, and his son Rajshekhar was married to the princess Shashiprabhá.

It so happened that another man from the city, Veer son of Dhana Sen, saw Shashiprabhá and was smitten by desire. He fell into a fever and would not even eat. Yasho Devi was his mother. She asked him what was the matter, and he told her all in a voice choked with emotion. 'The question is this,' the parrot added. 'She is a princess, and hard to get. So, how will he live?'

'You tell us,' said the merchant's wife. 'Prabhávati,' the parrot replied, 'I will tell you if you do not go out tonight.' 'Tell us!' she insisted, and here is the rest of the story.

Yasho Devi made friends with a bitch by feeding and petting it and suchlike. Ornamenting it with jewellery, she then took it with herself on a visit to Shashiprabhá. When she was alone with the princess, she said in melting tones: 'Both of us and this bitch were sisters in our previous lives. You and I satisfied our desires for men other than our husbands, I without any misgivings and you with many. But this one never did any such thing. Because of her chastity she has only a memory of her previous life, but bears none of its consequences; and she has been born as a bitch. You have no memory as your scruples interfered with your lovemaking. But my recollection of our previous life is as unimpaired as my enjoyment was unrestrained. Seeing you and this bitch has filled me with sympathy, and so I have come here to tell you all this. One should always give to supplicants what they yearn for. One who gives thus receives all prosperity. As it is said,

> Those who live on alms beg not,[1]
> but rather cry from door to door:
> "Always give to supplicants,
> those who don't will end like us."'

Shashiprabhá burst into tears and embraced Yasho Devi. 'My good lady!' she cried, 'find me a lover too!'

Yasho Devi comforted Shashiprabhá and took her home, where she introduced the princess to her son. She did all this with the knowledge of Rajshekhar, who raised no objection, thinking that Yasho Devi was a friend of his wife; he had moreover been propitiated with gifts of money and other things.

'My beauty,' the parrot concluded, 'in this way Yasho Devi duped the prince and the princess with her superior intelligence, and accomplished her own objective. Go and get a lover if you have her wits. Otherwise go to sleep, big eyes, and do not expose yourself to ridicule.'

And Prabhávati went to sleep after listening to the parrot's tale.

Here ends the second tale of Shuka Saptati

3

Kutil and Vimal

Asked by Prabhávati on the following day, the parrot said: 'Go wherever it pleases your heart, my lady. There is nothing unusual in it if, like the king, you know how to protect yourself.'

'How was that,' Prabhávati asked, and the parrot narrated: There is a city called Vishálá. In it there was a king called Sudarshan and a merchant named Vimal. There also lived in the city a rogue named Kutil who wanted to gain possession of the merchant's two wives, seeing that they were fair and beautiful. To this end he prayed to the goddess Ambika and begged to be made to look like Vimal.

Having obtained Vimal's form, the rogue went to the merchant's house when the latter had gone abroad, and took possession of everything. He gained control over all the servants with favours and grants of money and, having contented the two wives with much honour, gifts and the like, commenced to enjoy them as he pleased. The household thought all the while that Vimal's sudden generosity was due to his having at last realised the impermanence of wealth.

When the true Vimal returned, the gatekeeper forbade his entry into the house on Kutil's orders. The merchant shouted outside that he had been defrauded by some great rogue, and his relatives and other curious people found him thus, screaming away. The merchants shut their shops, and together with them he went to the guards and the chief officers crying, 'O King, some great rogue has defrauded me!'

The king sent his officials to inspect the matter, and the rogue won them over with cash and other presents. After seeing this benefactor within the house, the officials declared that Vimal, the owner was present inside his residence; the great rogue was the one shouting outside.

Both the men were then brought before the king. No one could tell which of the two was the scoundrel and which the one aggrieved. Soon the pandemonium disrupted all normal business. It also brought the king into disrepute, for his merit lies in suppressing villains and protecting those who abide by the law. It is said:

> The fire which is kindled
> by the people's travails
> will not be quenched without consuming
> a king's dynasty, glory and life.

The king sat by himself and pondered a judgement between the two parties. 'Tell me,' said the parrot, 'how should he decide?' and continued the story.

At last the king found a way. He had the two wives of Vimal separated from each other, and asked each of them: 'What jewellery and money did your husband give you at the time of your marriage? What did he say? And what conversation did you have with him afterwards, on the bridal night? Who are your mother and father, and what is your family and clan?'

Both women told the king all that had happened at their weddings, what they had received, what had been said, and how they had slept that night. The king then questioned the two men while they wrangled with each other. The one who could recount what the two wives, Rukmini and Sundari, had said obviously spoke the truth. The other one was the rogue and the king exiled him. As for Vimal, he went home after being honoured in the royal assembly.

'Such was that great king's intelligence,' said the parrot, and after listening to the tale, Prabhávati retired to sleep.

Here ends the third tale of Shuka Saptati

4

The Disastrous Fate of Govinda

O n the next day Prabhávati once again asked the parrot, and the bird said: 'Do not disdain my counsel and go out, for good advice should be accepted even from a child.

> A brahmin, in times past, my lady,
> disdained the advice of elders,
> got married to a vishakanyá,
> and suffered a calamity.'

'How did this happen?' Prabhávati asked, and this is the story the parrot told her.

There is a dwelling place of brahmins called Somaprabha. In that settlement there lived a learned and pious brahmin named Som Sharma. His daughter was endowed with beauty and other excellent qualities but she was reputed to be a vishakanyá, a poison maiden, fatal for anyone who slept with her. For fear of this no one would marry her.

Going about the country in search of a son-in-law, Som Sharma came eventually to another settlement of brahmins called Janasthan. There he found a brahmin named Govinda who was both impecunious and a dolt. To this person he gave his daughter Mohini in marriage.

Govinda was fascinated by Mohini's beauty and charm. Disdaining his well-wishers, he married her despite their remonstrations. She was an intelligent woman, while he was very young and a fool. Soon she began to bemoan the waste of her beauty, charm and youth on a person like him.

> For the wife, a foolish husband;
> for the woman, an unskilled lover;
> for the generous, lack of wealth:
> all these cause much pain.

> To be away from home
> in the season of rains,
> to be poor when one is young,
> and to be separated
> when one is first in love:
> all three are very painful.

> A song which is sung
> by one who is tuneless,
> a poem recited
> without an occasion,
> and sex with a woman
> who does not want it:
> all three are very painful.

One day she said to her husband: 'Much time has passed since I came to you from my father's house. I would like to visit him, but only with you and not otherwise.' Govinda then procured a bullock cart and set forth with his wife.

On the way they met a brahmin named Vishnu. He was a well-spoken young man, bold and goodlooking too. Mutual attraction between him and Govinda's wife developed in no time. It is said,

> First, love is born at some encounter,
> then longings fill the mind,
> sleeplessness, a sense of languor,
> an indolence in all faculties,
> disinterest in other subjects,
> loss of shame, of reason too,
> of consciousness itself, and death:
> through these ten conditions
> pass all who are stricken
> by the flower arrows of Káma,
> the master bowman
> who reigns supreme.

Their newfound fellow traveller gave many gifts of betel leaves and nuts to the couple, and in this way won the trust of Govinda who was just a country bumpkin. 'Vishnu may think that I am much too preoccupied with my wife,' Govinda worried, and dismounting from the bullock cart, he made the other man sit in it instead.

Once inside, Vishnu made love to Mohini as soon as her husband was separated from them by wayside trees. He got the girl under his influence and obtained from her the details of her name, family and clan. When the husband rejoined them, Vishnu prevented him from getting back into the cart. Holding on to his wife, he also humiliated Govinda, calling him a thief.

In the ensuing scuffle with Govinda, Vishnu drove him off with the vishakanyá's help, and proceeded with her to his own home. Govinda followed behind. Passing a village on the way, he raised a hue and cry: 'Help me, people! This thief has taken my wife away. Save her!'

The village headman seized Vishnu and Mohini. On being interrogated Vishnu said: 'I married this girl. This traveller saw my wife on the road and wishes to gain possession of her.' Govinda too gave the same reply when questioned. Getting identical answers from both, the judge proceeded to enquire about their family and other particulars.

'How will the judge decide between these three?' the parrot asked, and then continued the story at Prabhávati's insistence.

'Since when have you been travelling together?' asked the judge. 'We came together this morning, after breakfast,' they replied. The judge then questioned each of the two brahmins separately. 'What did this woman have at breakfast?' he asked. Govinda knew what she had eaten, but the other man did not, and he was denounced by the judge.

The judge also gave a sermon to Govinda. 'This brahmin woman is no good,' he advised. 'Give her up quickly, for she will give you grief in both this and the next world. It is said,

> Those who are wise
> will have nothing to do
> with doctors given to drink,
> half-baked actors, foolish monks,
> cowardly soldiers, aged gallants,
> brahmins devoid of learning,
> a state without ministers
> ruled by a child,
> a friend with treacherous ways,
> and a wife proud of her youth,
> in love with another man.'

But Govinda was infatuated with his charmer. Upbraided by all good people, he nevertheless went off with her, and was killed on the way for her sake.

'Thus, my lady,' said the parrot, 'whoever disdains the advice of his elders ends in disaster like the brahmin Govinda.' And Prabhávati slept after listening to this story.

Here ends the fourth tale of Shuka Saptati

5

The Fish Which Laughed

On the following day Prabhávati again asked the parrot about going out. 'Go, my lady,' the bird replied, 'if you know how to answer difficult questions like that clever young girl in the king's assembly.' On Prabhávati's enquiry, the parrot then related a story:

There is a city called Ujjayini which was ruled by the king Vikramaditya. His queen Kámalilá was from a high patrician family. The king loved her exceedingly.

Once, when the king was dining with the queen, he had some roasted fish served to her. 'My lord!' she cried, 'these are men! I am unable even to look at them, much less to touch them!' Hearing this, the fish burst into such peals of laughter that it could be heard even by people in the city.

The king questioned his ministers, astrologers, soothsayers and other experts about what had caused the fish to laugh.

When none of them could give him an answer, he said to his chaplain, who was the head of all the brahmins: 'It is now for you to explain why these fish laughed. Otherwise you will be exiled from the country.'

The chaplain begged for five days' grace and went home gloomily. 'If he does not find an answer, he will get exiled,' said the parrot. 'The question is, how can he be saved? And this is what happened.'

The chaplain's daughter was a young but learned girl. 'Father,' she asked the dejected brahmin, 'why are you looking so distressed? What is the reason for this gloom? Educated people must hold the head high even in times of trouble. It is said,

> Not gloating in prosperity,
> nor grieving in adversity,
> in battle never cowardly:
> such a one, though seldom born,
> does the universe adorn.'

The brahmin related what had happened, from the beginning to the end. 'The king is exiling me,' he said, 'for,

> In this world there cannot be
> friendship, faith, fraternity
> with anyone, or true affection,
> much less with kings who're all deception.

'And, it is said,

> Did anyone ever see or know
> of hygiene in the common crow?
> in gamblers truth, in snakes forbearance,
> in women pause from concupiscence,
> in neuters calm, in drunks reflection,
> and in kings a friend's affection?

'What is more,

> One should not trust the natures
> of clawed or horned creatures,
> of rivers, of men bearing arms,
> nor of kings, or feminine charms.

> Hooded are both snakes and kings,
> and similar too in other things:
> the outward skin they can discard,
> their ways are crooked, tempers hard,
> and it takes a lot of pain
> their goodwill to ever gain.

> The sovereign, with a smile will slay;
> and villains, as they homage pay;
> by touch itself can elephants kill;
> as snakes while simply sniffing will.

'This king has turned against me even though I have served him since his childhood. So, if I want to stay alive, I must go into exile with the other brahmins. It is said,

> The clan has precedence, over the man,[1]
> and the village before the clan;
> renounce the village, for the land of your birth,
> but for yourself, the entire earth.'

'What you say is right, father,' the girl replied after listening to him, 'but a vassal without a lord gets no respect anywhere. As it is said,

> Even a common person can
> become noble by serving the king.
> But, removed from service, any man,
> even the noble, is a common thing.

> Kings will favour only him,[2]
> who is keeping close to them,
> though base and worthless he may be.
> For kings and damsels, generally,
> like creepers tend to cling to that
> which happens to be their side at.

> To the king the servants will
> keep coming closer, though he still
> may try to keep them at a distance.
> They will slowly seek ascendance:
> so to get whatever could
> be got from his moods, bad or good.

'And further,

> For scholars, craftsmen, soldiers and
> all those who service understand,
> and for high positions hope:
> without a king there is no scope.

> Strengthened by the expectations
> of noble birth and such considerations,
> to kings who do not supplicate:
> to live by begging is their fate.

> When affected adversely
> by sickness, stars or royalty,
> the stupid ones, who do not know
> of regimens, spells or policy,
> are bound to perish definitely.
> Father, it is always so.

'It is said,

> Tigers from the wild, and serpents,
> lions too, as well as elephants —
> see, by stratagem they are caught
> and in their captors' control brought:
> cannot smart and cautious men
> do the same with monarchs then?

'And further,

> A scholar only rises high
> when on the king he can rely
> The sandal tree thrives not until
> it's nurtured on Malaya's hill.

> When the king is pleased, this brings
> as gifts and benefits, many things:
> bright parasols and horses elegant,
> and always lively troops of elephant.

'The king respects you, father. You are the recipient of his favours. So do not get distressed on account of this enquiry. For,

> When kings have difficult work to do,
> are seized with doubts, misgivings too:
> of these one who can their minds free,
> will from that gain primacy.

'Therefore, father, calm yourself. Have your bath and dinner. Why the fish laughed is a question I will answer before the king.'

The chaplain went to the king and made a representation as advised by his daughter. The monarch was satisfied and sent for her. She pronounced a benediction, and said to him: 'Your Majesty, do not trouble brahmins for nothing. Did you ever see or hear of fish laughing in this way? Are you not ashamed of putting such a question to me, a frail girl? For the king is not an ordinary person like others. He has a divine status. You, moreover, like your name Vikramaditya, are a sun of valour, a scorcher of foes. It is said

> The person of the king was created
> with majesty from Indra, lord of heaven,
> splendour from Agni, god of fire,
> wrath from Yama, god of death,
> affluence from Kuber, god of wealth,
> charisma from Rama, and calm from Krishna.

'To quote the *Mahabharata*,

> O Bhima, do not scorn
> the lord of eleven armies:
> the provider of even five men
> has a nature more than human.

'My lord, how is it that you did not consider this matter yourself? For you are able on your own to clear up all doubts. But if you are curious to know if others have the answer, then listen,

> This queen, a lady highly chaste,
> did not touch the fish because
> they were male. And that, for certain,
> is the reason why they laughed.

> Reflect, O king, within your heart,
> upon the meaning of this verse.
> Or else, you are a fool. my lord,
> to question me again.

'Your Majesty,' the chaplain's young daughter concluded, 'the queen is so well protected that she does not even see the sun. How can there be any suspicion about her chastity?'

But even though the girl had indicated the reason for the fish's laughter through the purport of her verse, the king and all his learned men could not grasp it. Seeing the assembly bemused, she got up and withdrew.

'What happened next, I will tell you in the morning,' said the parrot. And, having listened to the story, Prabhávati went to sleep.

Here ends the fifth tale of Shuka Saptati

6

The Importance of Keeping a Secret

'Parrot!' Prabhávati asked the bird on the next day, 'Did the king finally learn the secret of why the fish had laughed?'

'The king had no sleep that night,' said the parrot, 'for he could not understand the purport of the verse which had been recited to him. It is said,

> How can they sleep, lady,
> those who are tortured
> by illness or debt,
> who make many enemies,
> or when their spouses are
> out of control?'

Sleepless, the king spent a miserable night. In the morning he summoned the scholar maid and said: "I did not understand the meaning of that stanza. Therefore will you please explain why the fish had laughed?"

"Do not ask me, O king," she replied. "For you will regret it just like the merchant's wife who insisted that her husband tell her where the cakes came from."

"How did that happen?" asked the king, and this is the tale he was told.

There is a town hereabouts called Jayanti. In it there lived a man of the merchant caste named Sumati together with his dear wife Padmini. As this merchant's store of merits accumulated from his previous birth declined, so did his wealth; and people began to shun him, for men are friends only of money. It is said,

> He who has money has friends,
> he has relatives, is considered wise;
> one with money is regarded
> as a real man in this world.

And in the *Mahabharata*,

> The poor, the sick and the stupid,
> the slaves and those in exile:
> these five, O prince, are rated
> as dead even though they are alive.

And further,

> In this world, even strangers
> treat the wealthy as their own;
> but for the poor, within a moment,
> even relatives turn adverse.

So the merchant would bring items like grass and wood, and sell them in the city centre for a living. Once he was unable to obtain any of these things in the forest. All he could find was a sturdy wooden image of the god Ganesh, the remover of obstacles. 'What can I do with this?' he wondered. It is said

> What sins will the starving not commit?
> Hungry men turn pitiless too.
> They do what they must to stay alive,
> good people's ways are not for them.

As he lifted up the image in order to break it into bits, the god was pleased with him and said: 'Go to my temple at dawn. I will give you every day five cakes prepared with ghee and brown sugar. But you must not reveal this secret to anyone at all. If you do, this pledge will no longer hold good.'

Sumati agreed. Every day he would bring five cakes thus, and give them to his wife, who would feed their family with these divine sweetmeats made with brown sugar and ghee. She would also send some to the homes of their kinsmen, as also for the delectation of her girl friend Mandodari.

Once, when the girlfriend asked her, Padmini said that she did not know where the cakes came from. 'My dear!' the friend remarked slyly, 'where is our love for each other if you will not tell me your secrets? It is said,

> To give and to take a gift,
> to tell and to ask for a secret,
> to please and to enjoy each other:
> these are the six signs of love.'

'My husband has never told me this secret though I have asked him hundreds of times,' Padmini replied. 'If you cannot find it out,' her friend observed, 'then your life, beauty, youth, your everything is just meaningless.'

'How do you get these cakes?' Padmini then asked Sumati. 'By the grace of providence,' he told her, 'it is said,

> From another island though it be,
> from the ends of the earth or deepest sea,
> a favourable fate will swiftly bring
> and join to you your favoured thing.

'Furthermore,

> A mouse at night once made a hole
> and entered a reed basket, where
> it fell of itself into the jaws
> of a serpent which was there confined,
> with hunger weak, its organs failing;
> then, by the mouse flesh fortified,
> the snake escaped immediately
> through that very hole and fled.
> Be calm, therefore, its fate alone
> that causes men to rise or fall.'

Not getting an answer from her husband, Padmini decided to go on a fast unto death. 'If I talk about this,' the merchant explained, 'it will harm us and we will regret it greatly.' But when she continued to insist despite his adjurations, he told her, for destiny had impaired his intelligence. It is said,

> The man for whom the gods ordain
> destruction, they first take away
> his mind, so that he knows no more
> what is in his own interest.

"And relieved of his reason, King Vikramaditya, this man made the secret known," the scholar maid narrated. "It is said,

> Even good people generally
> lose their wits when trouble comes:
> Rama misjudged the deer of gold;[1]
> Nahush yoked brahmins to his car;
> Kartavirya was fool enough
> to carry off cattle from a priest;
> and Dharma's son did stake his queen
> and four brothers in the game of dice."

Having learnt the secret from her husband, Padmini told it to her friend who promptly sent her own husband with an axe to the statue of Ganesh. Sumati too went there in the morning. The god caught both of them in a magic noose. 'You wretch!' he said to Padmini's spouse, 'this mischief is your doing. It is you, therefore, who deserve to be punished.' Meanwhile the husband of Padmini's friend had made a supplication, and the god presented him with the five cakes.

Both men returned to their respective homes. 'You have done us out of the five cakes,' Sumati told his wife, 'and had them given to this woman!' And Padmini was stricken with remorse.

"It will be the same for you, great king," said the scholar maid. "Do not question me or you will regret it. So think by yourself about my verse." And she arose and went home.

After listening to this tale, Prabhávati went to sleep.

Here ends the sixth tale of Shuka Saptati

7

The Importance of Keeping
a Secret-II

'Once more, parrot,' Prabhávati asked the bird on the following day, 'did the king get to hear or come to know why the fish had laughed?'

'In the morning,' replied the parrot, 'the king summoned the scholar maid again, and said: "Why did those fish laugh? Tell me quickly, girl!"

"Do not insist, Sire," she responded, "otherwise you will regret it like the brahmin who was infatuated with the courtesan in times bygone."

There is, upon this earth, a city called Vatson which was ruled by the king Veer. A brahmin named Keshav lived there. Once he said to himself: 'I will not live on my father's wealth. It is held that

> The best people are known by their own merit,
> the middling by that of their fathers;
> the base are known by the uncle maternal,
> and the worst because of the father-in-law.

'What is more,

> Who becomes not parasitic
> with money by his father earned?
> Rarely is a person born
> who earns and spends himself.'

After coming to this conclusion, Keshav went about the country, through cities, cemeteries and holy places, in search of wealth. One day, tired after traversing a desolate region, at a famous altar to the god Shiva in a cemetery dedicated to the goddess Karálá, he saw an ascetic in deep meditation, squatting in a yogic posture upon a pale coloured tortoise. He stood before this personage, with hands folded in prayer, till the ascetic slowly came out of the trance and said: 'O what is to be given at this moment, and to whom? Who should be rescued from the ocean of this worldly round, and which is the guest whose problems should be solved?'

'I am your guest,' said Keshav the brahmin, raising his arm, 'and I seek wealth. It is said,

> Ready to give their own lives,
> such men are deeply saddened
> to see poor, honest people as supplicants,
> begging for small sums.

'What is more,

> Good people help others, even though
> themselves consumed by misfortune:
> like the sandal tree which cools
> others, itself getting chopped into bits.'

The great ascetic gave the brahmin some vermilion secreted at his side. 'When you touch this,' he told Keshav, 'it will always give you five hundred pieces of gold. But you must never talk about it or give it to anyone. Otherwise it will revert and return to me.'

Whenever the brahmin touched that gift it would give him five hundred gold coins in the morning. He went to the town of Ratnávati and there began an affair with a prostitute named Sthagiká. She on her part had no knowledge of where his money came from.

'This brahmin has no occupation or any such thing, dear,' Sthagiká's procuress asked her one day, 'from where does he get the money which he spends on us to enjoy himself?'

The prostitute asked the brahmin, but he never said anything. Then she pleased him with all her artful services and, on being questioned, he told her that the money came from the vermilion. She took it away while he was asleep, and the procuress turned him out of the house for being without money. It is said,

Is there any skill
in cheating one who trusts you?
And is it brave to kill
one who sleeps in your arms?

Not finding his vermilion, the brahmin went shouting to the
royal palace. 'I have been robbed!' he cried. Then there was
a hearing.

'This accusation is unfair,' the procuress pleaded, 'this
scoundrel has no money, but he lusts after my daughter because
he is smitten by Káma.'[1] The king could hardly understand
something difficult for even wise people to comprehend,
but what was established was that the money came from the
vermilion. The people expelled Keshav on learning that he
was an alien, and the magic vermilion returned to the great
ascetic.

"King Vikramaditya!" the scholar maid concluded, "by
falling in love with Sthagiká and telling her the secret of the
vermilion the brahmin was left with neither the one nor the
other. Your love and happiness too will be similarly affected."
And she went home.

Prabhávati listened to this tale and went away to sleep.

Here ends the seventh tale of Shuka Saptati

8

Do Not Insist Too Much

Asked again by Prabhávati on the following day, the parrot said: 'My lady, at their next meeting the girl scholar told the king: "Sire, it is not appropriate to keep on insisting. For,

> In no works should the king insist,
> auspicious or otherwise;
> for the royal persona is immense
> and the people are its parts —
> so what he does affects them all.

"If I tell you the answer," she added, "O king, you will find yourself in the same situation as the merchant's wife, who was left neither here nor there."

"How did that happen?" asked the king, and the scholar maid narrated:

In a place called Tripur, which was ruled by the king Trivikram, there lived a merchant named Sundar. His wife

Subhaga was the very opposite of chaste. She would go roaming outside the house and it was only with much effort that her husband could restrain her. Before he did so, another merchant made love to this libidinous woman regularly in the temple of the Yaksha.

Once, when her husband stopped her from going out, Subhaga told a girlfriend: 'Please get that man to the yaksha' temple today, my friend, so that I may go there and make merry with him. And, after I leave, please set fire to my house so that the people here are preoccupied and do not get to know that I have gone. Meanwhile I will have come back after enjoying myself.'

The other man came to the temple after receiving the message from the girlfriend. Subhaga also went there, and her friend set fire to her house after she had departed. But her lover left the temple out of curiosity to see the fire, and Subhaga's plan could not be consummated. By the time she returned, her house had burnt down.

"Great king," the scholar maid said in conclusion, "it is quite certain that what befell the merchant's wife will also happen to you: neither happiness at home, nor any outside. If you are nevertheless interested to know the meaning of that verse, I will myself explain it to you tomorrow." Saying this, she went home. Prabhávati, on her part, went to sleep after listening to this story.

Here ends the eighth tale of Shuka Saptati

9

Do Not Insist Too Much-II

Filled with wonder, Prabhávati asked the bird on the following day: 'Parrot! Did Vikramaditya learn the reason for the fish's laughter?'

'My lady, the king learnt nothing on his own,' the parrot replied. 'He summoned the brahmin's clever young daughter the next morning, and said: "You told me that I will understand this by myself. But I have understood nothing."

"Since the king has not understood even when I explained it, then listen," said the girl. "The minister Pushpahása, who is the chief among all your ministers, is in prison for no fault. Why has he been incarcerated?"

"This Pushpahása is like his name," the king replied. "Whenever he laughs there is a rain of flowers. This became well-known in other kingdoms, and they sent their men to investigate the marvel. But when they arrived here, he would not laugh and there was no floral shower. Because of this he was put into gaol."

"But why did he not laugh? Did you ascertain the reason?" the scholar maid asked. "I did not learn anything about it," said the king.

"In that case are you not culpable for punishing him in this way?" the maid retorted. "It is said,

> By law is a kingdom obtained,
> by law should it be nurtured,
> through law is the king its protector
> and the remover of every fear.

"Just as you have insisted on asking why the fish laughed, so too find out why the minister did not. He will tell you the reason for both."

As advised by the girl, the king then reinstated the minister Pushpahása in office with a robe of honour, and asked him both questions. "Scandals in one's own house should never be spoken about," the minister said, "for,

> The wise man will not publicise
> his loss of wealth, his personal grief,
> misdemeanours in his home,
> his being duped or humiliated.[1]

"However the king's command is supreme, for

> Far from giving gracious orders
> with a kind and tender heart,
> the master may not even cast
> a loving look at those who sin:
> such is the glory that is the king,
> powered by the law, it eclipses
> earthly lights like sun and fire,
> surpassing even heaven's splendour.

"Therefore, I will tell Your Majesty," the minister said. "My wife was in love with another man, and I had come to know this. I did not laugh because of the grief it caused me."

After hearing this, the king looked at the queen and struck her with a nosegay of flowers he had in his hand. She pretended to swoon at the blow and, at that sight, Pushpahása began to laugh. Soon there was a pile of flowers before him.

The king comforted the queen and looked fixedly at the brahmin's daughter. "Why did you laugh at us?" he asked the minister angrily. The latter clasped his hands together in fearful entreaty, and said: "Sire, your queen does not faint even when she is caned at night by the grooms. But now she is in a swoon. That is why I laughed."

"Minister!" the king asked, incensed, "did you see or hear of this?"

"Indeed, I have seen it, master," the minister replied, "if you do not believe it, take off her bodice and see for yourself."

The king had this done, and then he understood everything. Still, he stared at Pushpahása and the brahmin's daughter. "What is this?" he asked. "Master," said the minister, "the laughter of the fish was explained to you in a secret way by this girl. I have made it plain."

The king dismissed the assembly. Apprehensive as well as relieved, both Pushpahása and the brahmin maid returned to their respective homes. A man was discovered in the queen's bureau. The king had him executed, and turned the queen out of the palace.

'You too, good lady,' the parrot said to Prabhávati, 'should not insist on something just like that. For one who keeps on insisting is liable to public embarrassment like Vikramaditya.' And Prabhávati slept after listening to this story.

Here ends the ninth tale of Shuka Saptati

10

Shringáravati Helps Her Co-Wife

'What should I do, parrot?' asked Prabhávati, all dressed up. 'Today, you tell me. You say such nice things.'

'Go,' said the bird, 'if you have a friend like Shringáravati to help you.'

'What is this story?' Prabhávati enquired, and this is what the parrot narrated.

In a place called Rajpur there lived the householder Devasákhya with his two wives Shringáravati and Subhaga. Both ran after other men and were famous for their lovemaking. They were also adept in ways of protecting each other.

Once, while Subhaga was inside the house with a lover, her husband arrived at the gate from abroad, a barleria[1] plant in his hand.

'What happens to her now is the question,' the parrot said, and continued the tale.

Shringáravati stripped Subhaga naked and turned her out of the house. 'What has happened?' the husband asked, to which Shringáravati replied with all respect: 'As you have brought this barleria from the grove of the goddess Devi, Subhaga has become possessed by that divinity. Please go and return the plant to its proper place, so that her health may be restored.'

And, as that ignoramus of a husband went back to replace the plant, Shringáravati enabled the lover to escape also.

After listening to this story, Prabhávati retired to bed.

Here ends the tenth tale of Shuka Saptati

11

How Rambhika Had Her Way

The charming Prabhávati continued to be distracted by thoughts of love. 'I will go if you agree,' she said to the parrot respectfully, the next evening.

'You should certainly go,' the parrot replied. 'That is my definite view, for who can prevent the mind from seeking what it wants and water from flowing downwards. But, if you go you must be prepared to do something out of the ordinary, as Rambhika did in times past for the sake of the brahmin.'

On Prabhávati's enquiry, the parrot then narrated this tale.

There is a village called Dábhila of which the headman was one Vilochan. His wife Rambhika wanted other men, but none would reciprocate her desires for fear of her husband. So she picked up a pitcher and went to the village well on the pretence of fetching water. There she saw a traveller, a handsome brahmin youth, and gave him a look which signalled a proposition for making love. He too grasped her intention,

for he was a clever fellow who understood feminine glances.
It is said,

> Signals are caught even by beasts,
> horses and elephants bear loads when urged;
> the wise can infer even the unsaid,
> to understand hints is a fruit of wit.

And,

> Rolling the pelvis, and looking at you
> repeatedly with a lovelorn gaze:
> you simple boy, what has she not
> already told you thus?

> The man who cannot comprehend
> the heart's desire long conveyed
> through a woman's eyes: what can
> explaining do for such a fool?

'What should I do, good lady?' the young brahmin said, going
up to Rambhika.

'Just follow me,' she said. 'We will go to my house, and
there you should salute my husband. All the rest I will do. You
have only to say, it is so.'

Speaking thus, she went inside the house. He entered also,
and found himself before her astonished husband. Meanwhile
she had put down the pitcher of water. Going up to her spouse
she said: 'Lord, look at him!'

'I do not know him,' said the husband. 'He is the son of my mother's sister,' she explained, 'I left him in childhood. His name is Dhaval, and he has come to meet me. After welcoming him with an embrace, I have been asking him about news of our relatives.'

'That is so,' muttered the brahmin. She then took him into the kitchen with her husband's permission, and entertained him with a new garment and a meal.

The husband was satisfied. 'Good woman,' he said, 'you must look after your cousin well.' And, with these words, he went off to sleep.

Rambhika then sat down on the bed prepared for the brahmin. 'You told your husband that your brother has come,' he said, 'and I have acknowledged you as my sister. An acceptance has to be honoured. It is said,

> Loss of life may come to pass,
> loss of freedom, loss of wealth:
> the good will always keep their word,
> whatever else will be, will be.[1]

> My beauty, you must never do,
> at stake though life itself may be,
> that which puts the heart to shame,
> and tarnishes your family's name.'

'Don't speak like this,' said Rambhika,

> For it is very hard to find
> a girl devoted to one's parents;
> and men who have the same devotion
> should take pleasure in that girl.

'And it is said,

> When a damsel, moved by Káma,
> herself approaches a man,
> and he does not make love to her;
> then, stricken by her sighs, he will
> for certain be consigned to hell.

'Why should anyone who accepts this consider any woman as forbidden? So, do not reject my love,

> It is heard that, in times past,
> Krishna took the lovesick Rukmini
> though she was his brother's wife:[2]
> who indeed may transgress Káma?

> Even Brahma was moved by Káma,
> and lusted after his own daughter:
> he still shines, with form enchanting,
> in heaven, to this very day.
> Even Shiva's seed was spilt
> when at their wedding he beheld
> that Parvati was drawn to him:
> and thus were born the Bályákhilyas.'[3]

But when the fool would not make love to Rambhika even after all that she had said, she began to scream: 'Help! Help! I am being raped!' And, as she screamed, her husband came running with his relatives, shouting 'What is it?'

'How will the brahmin be saved? This is the question,' said the parrot, 'and here is the answer.'

The terrified brahmin bowed down and fell at Rambhika's feet. 'Mistress!' he cried, 'save my life! I will do whatever you wish.' She then slopped some milk and rice under the bed and quickly lit a fire nearby. 'He has cholera!' she told her husband who had just come in, 'that is why I screamed.' She pointed out the mess of milk and rice to her foolish spouse, who looked at it and went out again. And when he had gone to sleep, she made love with the brahmin at her pleasure. He stayed with her for a month on the pretext of convalescence, after which he went home.

Having listened to this story, Prabhávati again retired to bed.

Here ends the eleventh tale of Shuka Saptati

12

Shobhika Saves Her Lover

On the following day the parrot told Prabhávati as she was about to go out: 'Will you know what to say in a crisis, as did Shobhika when her lover climbed up the acacia tree?'

In the village of Nalauda there lived a potter who was very rich. His wife Shobhika was supremely unchaste and lustful of men. She would dally in the house with a lover whenever her husband went out. Once the potter came home while she was thus occupied. 'What will happen to her is the question,' said the parrot, and continued the story.

As soon as she realised that her husband had returned, Shobhika told her paramour: 'Climb up that acacia tree.' He did as he was advised, but while scrambling up the tree the sole garment that he was wearing fell off, so that he got to the top stark naked.

'What is this?' asked the potter, when he saw a naked man on the tree. 'He was being chased by enemies,' his wife explained. 'So he climbed up the acacia in a hurry, dropping even his dhoti in the process.'

Shobhika's husband brought the man down slowly from the tree and sent him home, while that wily woman clapped and laughed.

After listening to this story Prabhávati retired to sleep.

Here ends the twelfth tale of Shuka Saptati

13

Rajika Finds an Excuse

Asked by Prabhávati on the next day, the parrot said: 'Go and enjoy yourself, my lady, and give a considered answer as did the dust covered Rajika to her husband who was waiting for his dinner.'

There was a merchant who lived in a place called Nagpur. His wife Rajika was good to look at but bad in her ways. The merchant did not know that she was involved with another man.

Once, as her husband sat down for his dinner, Rajika saw her lover passing by on the road. The man made a sign to her, at which she got up, saying: 'There is no ghee at home today.' Taking some money from her husband, she went out of the house on the pretext of getting ghee, but stayed outside for a long time with her boyfriend. As for the husband, he was left at home, fuming and famished.

The question is: how did she come home? And the answer: she came back with her hands, feet and face covered with grime, and the money dust smeared as well.

'What is this?' asked her husband, his eyes red with anger. 'Your money, for which you are so angry,' she said, showing him a heap of dust as she wept and sighed, 'it fell into this dirt. Take it and toss it clean.'

The merchant was embarrassed. He dusted his wife's limbs with his own shawl and comforted her with many endearments.

Prabhávati went to sleep after listening to this story.

Here ends the thirteenth tale of Shuka Saptati

14

Dhanashri's Hair Braid

'Well, big eyes,' said the parrot on the following day, as Prabhávati was stepping out, 'it is all right doing what you please and making love with another man. But you should know, like Dhanashri, what to say should the husband turn up on the scene.'

'What is this story?' asked that round-hipped beauty, and here it is.

In the city of Padmavati there lived a merchant named Dhanapál whose wife Dhanashri was dearer to him than even his own life. The couple enjoyed themselves in their mutual affection.

Once the merchant took his money and went abroad after consulting his wife. After he had gone, Dhanashri remained at home without any zest for life. She would not eat or gossip with her friends. She stopped bathing, gave up wearing ornaments and became indifferent even to her own person.

Time passed, and then it was spring. It is the king of the seasons, and comes upon the earth riding on the southern breezes. The call of the koels is its fanfare, the buzz of the bees its marching song, and the fragrance wafting from the jasmine its herald. Its arrival distracts even the most disciplined of minds.

Dhanashri stood on the roof of her house at the time of the spring festival, and cursed her own youth and comeliness as she gazed at the merriment in the city. 'My beauty,' said a girlfriend who sensed her feelings, 'do not let your looks and years go waste. For

> Listen, you lovely-legged girl,
> spring has sounded on the earth
> Káma's royal proclamation
> with the koel's song:
> let gallants all shed haughtiness
> and enjoy their mistresses;
> for youth is transient in this world
> and life itself is fleeting.

'So you too should seek the fulfilment of your youth.'

'I cannot wait anymore,' said Dhanashri. 'Do whatever you can.' The girlfriend then introduced her to another man. And when he discovered that Dhanashri had become infatuated with him, he cut off one night the single braid in which she wore her hair as was the custom for women whose husbands were away.

Dhanashri's husband happened to return from abroad at that time. 'What will she do now, is the question,' said the parrot, and proceeded to give the answer.

When Dhanapál arrived at the gate, Dhanashri had already thought out what to do. 'Lord,' she said, 'you must stay at the gate while I get everything organised.' As he waited, she went inside, prayed to the household goddess and placed her braid of hair before the deity. Coming out, she led her husband in together with the cake offering and said: 'Lord, worship our household goddess.'

While making his devotions, the husband saw the braid of hair. 'What is this?' he asked. 'I had made a vow,' she said, 'that when my husband comes back, I will cut off my braid before our lady. This is what I have done.' And that simpleton bowed to the goddess and lauded his wife.

Once again Prabhávati retired to sleep after listening to the story.

Here ends the fourteenth tale of Shuka Saptati

15

The Ordeal of Shreyá Devi

On the following day, as Prabhávati was leaving, the parrot laughed and said: 'Carry on, if you know what to say as Shreyá Devi did when her anklet was stolen.'

In the city of Shálipur there lived the merchant Sháliga and his spouse Jayati. They had a son named Gunákar, and Shreyá Devi was his wife. She was having an affair with another merchant called Subuddhi but, though this had already become notorious, her husband paid no attention to the gossip as he was in love with her. It is said,

> Those who love, look for merits,
> those displeased, look for faults,
> and the men in the middle
> are interested in both.

What is more,

> Men in love, even though smart,
> can never control themselves;
> the others, young women can catch
> no more than water in the hand.

Once Shreyá Devi's father-in-law saw her asleep with the other man, and took off the anklet from her foot. She realised what had happened, and sent her lover to fetch her husband with whom she then went to bed. Later, waking him up from his sleep, she said: 'Your father took off my anklet and has it. Such an improper act has never been known before: a father-in-law removing an anklet from the foot of a daughter-in-law!'

'I will get it in the morning from my father,' said Gunákar, 'and return it to you myself.' The next day he berated his father and asked for the ornament.

'I saw her asleep with another man,' the father explained, 'that is why I took the anklet.'

'But I was sleeping with your son!' Shreyá Devi protested. 'I will undergo the sacred ordeal to prove this. A yaksha[1] is located in the north of this very town. I will pass through between his legs. It is well-known that only those who speak the truth can do so and come out.'

The father-in-law agreed. That hussy then went to her lover's house while it was still day, and told him: 'Darling, in the morning I will perform the ordeal of passing between the yaksha's legs. You must come there, pretend to be mad, and clasp my neck.'

Shreyá Devi returned home after speaking to her lover. In the morning she assembled all the leading citizens and proceeded to the yaksha's temple with rice, flowers and other material for the ritual. Having bathed in the nearby lake, as she entered the temple to worship the yaksha, her lover put both his arms around her neck and behaved crazily as previously arranged.

'Oh, what is this!' cried Shreyá Devi, and went back to bathe again while the people caught hold of the make-believe madman and drove him away. Returning after her ablution, she went up to the yaksha, worshipped the deity with flowers, incense and suchlike, and cried aloud in everyone's hearing: 'O lord yaksha! If any man other than my husband and this lunatic has ever touched me, may I not be able to pass between your legs.'

In the presence of all the people she then entered between the yaksha's legs and came out safely. The deity stayed still, praising her intelligence in his own mind. And all the people lauded her as a chaste and holy lady, before they returned home.

'Go, if you know how to act like Shreyá Devi,' said the parrot. And, after listening to the bird, Prabhávati went to sleep.

Here ends the fifteenth tale of Shuka Saptati[2]

16

The Mutual Lockout

'Parrot, I will go to some other man,' Prabhávati said as she was leaving the next day. 'What you say is right enough,' the bird replied. 'One should act in accordance with one's heart. Those who cannot may be quite sorry like Mugdhika.'

'What is this story?' Prabhávati asked, and the parrot proceeded to narrate it.

In the city of Vidisha lived a merchant named Janavallabh, whose wife Mugdhika was wilful and wayward. Greatly shamed by her, he told his relatives that she slept outside, that is, carried on with other men.

When the relatives conveyed this to Mugdhika, she too retorted: 'He maligns me for nothing. It is he who sleeps around outside all the time.'

The relatives brought them together, and an agreement was made that whoever slept outside from that day would be at fault. Even after this pact, Mugdhika left her husband sleeping and went out.

After she had gone, her husband bolted the door from within before going back to sleep. When she returned from her tryst outside, and he would not open the door, she threw a rock into the well and just stood by the gate.

Thinking that his wife had fallen into the well, Janavallabh opened the door and came out. She meanwhile went in and shut the door behind her. Locked out, he began crying 'O darling!' and weeping loudly. Fearing that their secret would now become public, she then emerged and took her husband inside. The couple agreed that they would never again speak against one another.

Prabhávati went to bed after listening to this story.

Here ends the sixteenth tale of Shuka Saptati

17

The Smooth Talking Brahmin

O n the following day, when Prabhávati asked the parrot
with a laugh about going to another man, the bird said:
'Do just what your heart desires. It is said,

> Check out with a look[1]
> where you place the foot;
> with a filter of cloth
> the water which you drink;
> with the test of truth
> the words that you utter;
> and with your own heart
> the way you behave.

'But, gentle one, those who act as they feel should be able to
endure any problems that may arise, and also to speak up like
the brahmin Gunádhya.'

Iu the city of Vishálá there lived a brahmin named Yáyajuka with his very dear and fair wife Páhini. Their son was given the fullest education in proper order by his father, and one day he left his parents and went away to another country. Living by his wits in the town of Jayati, he became well-known under the name Gunádhya. He also kept a bull which he reared on barley, grass and such things.

The bull would follow Gunádhya everywhere. One day he put a harness on the animal and, assuming the garb of an itinerant trader, went to the procuress of the prostitute Madaná. 'Our bullocks will be coming with their loads in the morning,' he said to the go-between lady. 'Today I have come to get them fodder. The night I will spend wherever I can get a place to tether them.'

The procuress was interested in getting hold of any wealth the bullocks might be carrying, and agreed to take Gunádhya in. He tethered his bull and went up to the harlot who provided him with a bath and dinner.

Gunádhya was aroused, and spent the night with Madaná. The next day he was the first to get up in the morning, when he took the harlot's chain of gold and slipped away.

A servant girl also woke up as Gunádhya left. Seeing that the bull was no longer there, she called out to the procuress. 'What has happened, madam?' she asked, but the go-between, realising that the visitor had deserted Madaná, preferred to remain silent. It is said,

> The wise man will not publicise
> his loss of wealth, his personal grief,
> misdemeanours in his home,
> his being duped or humiliated.[2]

On another day Gunádhya was waylaid by the prostitute. He had lost a gambling match and still had the chalk marker in his hand. But he thought immediately of a way out. 'Procuress! Procuress!' he shouted, and afraid of the police, the harlot let him go. He then followed her, crying 'Procuress!' till they reached a quiet spot. There he placated her with the gift of a gold ornament from his hand.

> When things go counter to one's wishes,
> one who can bear and also concede them,
> will have his way; and never
> get blamed by good people.

Prabhávati retired to sleep after listening to this story.

Here ends the seventeenth tale of Shuka Saptati

18

The Ready Wit of the Mustard Thief

‹ ❦ ›

'Go, my lady,' said the parrot as Prabhávati was leaving the next day, 'you will not be faulted for going to the lover's house if you have brains in your head like the mustard thief.'

In the town of Shubhasthána there was a merchant named Daridra into whose house a thief once broke in. Unable to find anything there at all, he came out with a bunch of mustard stalks, in which condition he was apprehended by the police. They took him through the city with the stalks of mustard tied around his neck, and the question is how will he free himself from the authorities.

The answer is that to everyone who asked him, the thief would declare: 'Oh, there is nothing to this mustard!' 'I do not understand the intent of what you say,' the king told him after summoning him to the assembly. 'On the day of the annual sacrifice,' he replied, 'people tie five grains of mustard to their hands for warding off problems. From today this no longer holds good. For, with all this mustard tied around my neck, I still remain a prisoner.'

The king laughed on hearing this, and let the mustard thief go. As for Prabhávati, she went to sleep after listening to this story.

Here ends the eighteenth tale of Shuka Saptati

19

Santiká Saves Her Husband and His Lover

'Do as you please, delicate one,' the parrot said to Prabhávati as she was leaving, 'if you are as capable as Santiká who saved her husband and Svachhandá.'

There is a town called Karahad which was ruled by King Gunapriya, a lover of merits as his name indicates. In the same town lived a chief of the merchants named Sodhak with his wife Santiká, a chaste lady devoted to her husband.

Another merchant also lived there, but his wife Svachhandá was adulterous. She had always wanted Sodhak, but he would not respond to her desires. Once he went to the temple of the yaksha[1] Manoratha to pay his respects. Svachhandá followed him in and, seducing him with her coquettish ways, got him to make love to her. It is rightly said,

> Man stays on the path of virtue,
> keeps his urges under control,
> and bears shame and decorum in mind,
> only till some wanton beauty
> will let fall upon his heart
> the dark winged arrow of her glance,
> released from brows drawn to the ear,
> and shatter all his resistance.[2]

Seeing the couple so engaged, the royal guards surrounded the temple in order to arrest them. But Santiká realised that her husband was innocent, and went to the temple at night, beating a drum loudly. 'I have been observing a fast all day,' she told the guards, 'and only after beholding the yaksha will I eat by myself. Take some money and let me go in.'

The guards did as Santiká had asked. She then dressed Svachhandá to look like her, and sent that woman out while herself staying inside. In the morning the guards found the merchant with his own wife, and were greatly embarrassed.

After listening to this story Prabhávati went to sleep.

Here ends the nineteenth tale of Shuka Saptati

20

Kálika Dupes Her Spouse

'Go to the lover you fancy, my lady,' the parrot said, asked by Prabhavati on the next day, 'but only if you know like Kálika a wonderful way of hoodwinking husbands.'

At a place called Shankhapur by the side of the river Sábhramati,[1] there lived a rich farmer named Soora. His wife Kálika was both cunning and unchaste. She was having an affair with a brahmin who lived at Siddheshvarapur on the other bank of the river.

Infatuated with the brahmin, Kálika would go to him at night after crossing the river with the help of a messenger woman who was her neighbour. Her husband, the farmer, came to know of this one day. He went out to investigate what she was doing, and it so happened that when she came to the riverside she saw him there.

Kálika would habitually cross the river with the aid of a clay pitcher as a support. On this occasion she filled the pitcher with water, and used it to bathe and adorn the image of the goddess inside her neighbour's house. 'Mistress,' she said to the messenger woman, whom she had already alerted with a sign, 'you had earlier told me that if I do not bathe the goddess Siddheshvari my husband would die within five days. Now, if your word holds good, may my spouse live long.'

'So be it!' said the neighbour, and Kálika's husband quietly went away, fully satisfied with what he had heard.

After listening to this story, Prabhávati went to bed.

Here ends the twentieth tale of Shuka Saptati

21

The Intelligence of Mandodari

Questioned by Prabhávati on the following day, the parrot said: 'Go, my lady, there is no harm in going if you have the intelligence of Mandodari to help you in all that you do.' 'What is this story?' she enquired, and this is what the bird recounted.

There is a city called Pratishthan. The king there was Hemaprabha, and Shrutisheel was his minister. Yashodhar, the chief of the merchants' guild, lived there with his wife Mohini. Their daughter Mandodari had been given in marriage to Shrivatsa, another merchant who had come to Pratishthan from Kantipuri.

Mandodari and her husband were a most promiscuous couple. She used to sleep with a prince to whom she had been introduced by her neighbour, a worthless go-between woman named Damshtrakarálá to match her ugly teeth. Having become pregnant, Mandodari developed cravings which sometime occur in that condition, and killed the king's pet peacock for a meal.

The king was in the habit of having the peacock in attendance when he dined. The bird being untraceable at his dinner time on that particular day, a proclamation was made by beating the drum to ascertain its whereabouts. The go-between procuress then came forward and put her hand on the drum.

The procuress let it be known that someone with the cravings of pregnancy had eaten the peacock. The pregnant Mandodari was then asked, and she received the other woman with all respect when the latter came to her house. It has been said,

> Eight virtues need nurture by man:
> with girls, sweet flirtation;
> with gentlefolk courtesy;
> valour with enemies; kindness with elders;
> compliance with the knowledgeable;
> full ceremony with the proud;
> goodness with the good;
> and villainy with villains.

Mandodari however narrated the entire episode of the peacock to the treacherous procuress. It is said,

> Do not trust unreliable people,
> and not even those who are dependable:
> for the danger in the latter trusting
> can destroy one completely.[1]

One must keep some secrets
even from spouse, friend, and son;
the wise confide after much solicitation,
and serious thought if it will be proper.

What is more,

Even the cordial words of enemies
should in this world be judged with care;
the deer is caught by not giving thought
to the reason why its hunter sings.[2]

It is said even in the Kiráta,[3]

Those fools end in disaster
who deceive not the deceitful:
for the villains gain access like
sharp arrows to the body
which is left uncovered,
and will finish it off.

After getting to know all the details, the procuress reported them to the minister. The latter told the king, who observed:

Do not come easily to conclusions,
do not believe what you have not seen
with your own eyes; and even if you have,
consider its rights and wrongs.

'That man is the chief merchant of the city,' the king added. 'His daughter-in-law would never do such a thing. He must not be brought to ridicule until there is direct evidence.'

The minister explained all this to the procuress. She then hid him in a chest which she sent to Mandodari's house on the pretext of keeping it in the latter's custody. Going there herself, she told the girl: 'My dear, I admire you for eating that peacock. It is said that

> The peacock, quail and partridge,
> the blackbuck, deer and gazelle,
> the rhinoceros and the tortoise are
> the best of edible meats.'

She then asked Mandodari to repeat the whole story once again, and tapped on the chest in a signal to the minister to listen as the girl recounted it.

'How will the merchant's daughter-in-law get out of this predicament?' asked the parrot. 'And her father and father-in-law? It is said,

> Nothing good does ever come
> from associating with the base;
> for they only act wickedly
> even with those they like.

> The base know only how to spoil,
> not to help another's work;
> the rat's ability only lies
> in pilfering, not in guarding grain.

The good may even lose their lives
in the company of the bad:
just as the sesame seeds get ground
among the stones of the mill.'

'Mother,' the merchant's girl said carefully, even as the procuress tapped the chest with her hand, 'by the time I had done all this, the night was over, and I woke up. So I did not see anything further. Such was the dream I had, mother, and you must now say what it means for me!'

Having listened to this conversation, the minister opened the lid of the chest and came out. The merchant's daughter-in-law was duly honoured by him, and the procuress was exiled.

Prabhávati retired to sleep after listening to this story.

Here ends the twenty-first tale of Shuka Saptati

22

The Farmer's Wife

'Go, my lady,' said the parrot when questioned by Prabhávati yet again. 'My view is that you should certainly go if you have an answer like the one given by Madhuká.'

'How did that happen?' Prabhávati asked, and the bird related the following tale.

There was a farmer named Sodhak who lived in the village of Dambhila. Madhuká was his wife. She would take rice for his meal every day, and on the way be enjoyed by another man named Surapal, who came from elsewhere. One day she left the food on the road while she was with her lover, and a rogue called Muladeva put inside the rice an ushtriká, which is a camel-shaped clay flask for wine.

Madhuká took the container of rice without opening it. But when her husband saw the ushtriká inside and asked why it was there, she came up with an immediate answer. 'Lord,' she said, 'last night I dreamt that you had been devoured by an ushtriká, that is, a she camel. I have done this to counter that bad omen. Have this meal with a calm mind so that all possible mishaps can be averted.'

After listening to Madhuka's explanation, her besotted husband consumed even the ushtriká. And, after hearing this tale, Prabhávati went to sleep.

Here ends the twenty-second tale of Shuka Saptati

23

The Clever Procuress

Urging her to go out and take a lover, Prabhávati's friends told her on the following day:

'When trickling drops of perspiration
wash off the sandal paste from breasts;
when tinkling anklets can't be heard
amidst the moans, in love's contest;
when all the amorous acts occur
with promptitude, in harmony;
that, I hold, is love's true pleasure
the rest, my friend, is nature's course.'

'Similarly,

Life is not fulfilled for one
who will not take a risk for love;
that alone is love, it's said,
whose coming brings one joy supreme.

> Health be it, or happiness,
> pleasure, zest or affluence:
> all of them are meaningless
> unless enjoyed with one you love.'

'And it is said,

> Her eyes grew wide with joy to see[1]
> herself so splendid in the mirror,
> and Párvati could wait no longer
> to go to Shiva: the ornaments
> of women are for lovers' eyes.'

But the parrot quoted from the book of proper conduct:

> 'It is always easy to find[2]
> people who speak sweetly, O King;
> of that which is wholesome but bitter,
> both speaker and listener are rare.'

'There is no need to say much to you and to all these experts in what should or should not be done,' the parrot continued. 'But listen to this tale of the procuress, and then consider if you should leave in a hurry.'

There is a city called Padmávati. Its streets were paved with precious stones, and looked so splendid in the sunlight that it seemed as if the glow of jewels from the divine serpent Sesha's hood had spread upon the earth.

The king of this city was named Sudarshan. The kings Kusha and Bali could not have exceeded him in wealth and charity, nor the gods Hari and Shashi in strategy and pleasantness. He was a true protector of the people, and faults had disappeared from his kingdom like darkness in daylight. He enjoyed himself with his wife Shringára Sundari.

One day summer arrived:

> The sun is sharp, the wind is hot,
> the days are long and hard to bear;
> such is summer, everything
> then turns harsh, my dear.
>
> But summer can be overcome
> with use of sandal paste and pure
> drinking water, cold and clear,
> and sweet withal; not otherwise.
>
> Even summer is their slave,
> who avail of sandal paste at noon,
> who bathe again at eventide,
> and use the fan for breeze at night.

Such was the summer when a merchant named Chandra sat on the roof of his house with his wife Prabhávati. The sun, unable to cling to the sky despite its beams, was setting in the western sea. It is said

> Means, though many, turn futile
> when fate becomes adverse:
> even its thousand beams and rays
> cannot uphold the setting sun.

The sun's rays had disappeared, and only a red glow remained. Its orb shone like a globe of coral fallen from the evening maiden's hand. Meanwhile the moon had arisen on the eastern hillcrest, its beams poised like warriors to strike at their enemy, darkness. The moon gleamed like a lamp in the dark that evening, or like a black spotted disc in the lap of the damsel of the night.

The merchant would make love to his wife on such evenings, and a son was born to them in due course. Named Rama, he was given the fullest education by his father.

'I have only one son,' Chandra's wife told him once, 'I feel extremely sad because of that.'

'Even one son is good for you,' Chandra replied. 'It is said

> Clever, sweet and generous,
> serious, skilled and virtuous,
> even one such son is preferable.

'For

> What is the point of many sons,
> if they cause grief and regret?
> Better is just one who will help
> the family and bring it credit.'

Having said this, the merchant summoned the procuress Dhúrtamáyá and told her: 'I will give you a thousand pieces of gold if you make my son versed in the mysteries and deceptions of women.'

The procuress having agreed and promised to do what he had requested, the merchant assigned Rama to her in front of witnesses, stipulating, 'If my son is defrauded by even one courtesan, I will take twice as much gold from you.' Dhúrtamáyá agreed to this too and, having made a written contract, Chandra sent the lad to her house.

Rama began to study with Dhúrtamáyá the various artifices perfected by courtesans: the affected language of harlotry; the false promises, the devious ways, the genteel begging; the simulation of emotions with make-believe tears and laughter; and fictitious grief and joy which mean nothing. Also, the affection and the artless simplicity of these charmers; their equanimity in happiness and sorrow, virtue and sin; and the techniques of duplicity they reveal before their lovers. For lip and hand, cheek and bosom, the zone of the navel and that of the pubes, are the same in all women; but the heart of each is unique.

After Rama had thus been trained in all the practices of courtesans, the procuress took him back to his father as she had promised. On Chandra's orders the youth was then sent to the island of Suvarnadvipa on a trading mission.

In Suvarnadvipa there was a courtesan named Kalávati. Rama stayed with her for a year while she practised her arts on him. But he would tell her: 'Show me something special. This, even my younger sister has told me about.' When Kalávati was unable to lay hands on his wealth despite all her harlotry, she reported everything to her mother who was also her keeper.

'He is definitely the son of a courtesan,' said the mother.
'You will not be able to get hold of his money in this way. It
can only be acquired by some stratagem. So, when he starts
wanting to return home and asks for your permission, you
should tell him: "I too will go with you. If you do not take
me I will kill myself." You should then jump into the well.
This is bound to make such an impression upon him that he
will give you everything.'

'Mother!' said Kalávati, 'of what use will his money be if
I am not alive? It is said

> One should not even think of money
> which can only be acquired
> by transgressing dharma's law,
> by surrendering to the enemy,
> or by taking so much trouble
> that it ceases to be worthwhile.'

'Do not speak like that, my dear,' her mother replied, 'money
which can lead to death will also save life. It is said,

> Nothing good can be obtained
> without resort to enterprise:
> that man attains the finest fortune
> who is courageous in all his work.

> Like fishermen, one cannot win
> a great fortune without performing
> difficult deeds: like piercing someone
> else's gullet and killing him.

> Fate alone makes things to be
> smooth or difficult; causes
> humiliation or respect;
> makes men donors or beggars.

'Fear not, moreover, for I will spread a net inside the well.'

After listening to her keeper Kalávati did as she was advised, and Rama gave her all that he possessed. Having taken the money which amounted to a million, she threw him out in disgrace. It is said,

> Harlots indeed make love to men,
> but for money they cheat even the ones
> they love; keep away from them for
> they love not even themselves.

Having lost his money as well as his reputation, Rama boarded someone else's ship and returned home. Chandra was in tears to see his only son, now destitute of resources and retainers. He asked the boy how he had come to this pass, and the latter was so ashamed that he had the situation explained to his father through the family counsellor.

'Do not get dejected, my boy,' said the father, 'both adversity and prosperity come man's way. As it is said,

> Why worry so, O lordly elephant,
> why close your eyes in grief
> at separation from your herd?
> Eat and drink what you are given,
> for it is fate alone which brings
> prosperity or adversity.

What is this quicksilver wealth
for the high minded man?
Its loss leads but to sorrow,
and its coming only to joy.'

Having comforted his son with such words, the merchant
sent for Dhúrtamáyá. 'Here is a wonder which has come to
pass,' he said to her, 'even though my son was entrusted to
you for his training, he has come back after losing all his
money.'

'Who has not been deceived by women?' the procuress
replied. 'It is said,

Who turns not proud on getting rich,
and has no trouble when seeking pleasure?
Who has not been deceived by women?
And who indeed is dear to kings
in this world, or free of death?
Which beggar ever gains respect?
And, into evil company fallen,
who can come out safe and sound?

In the hills and forests dense
which comprise the feminine form,
Káma the thief has put to shame
Vishnu and Shiva, god and man'

'Now you should load another ship and send me there with
your son,' the procuress added. 'It is said,

> You should do what's done to you,
> if you are hit, then hit right back;
> if he plucks feathers from my wing,
> the hair I'll pull out from his head.'

'I had told you that if your son is cheated by any woman at all, it will be my responsibility. It is said,

> The earth may waiver, though supported
> by holy mountains, cosmic elephants,
> and the tortoise god and serpent;
> but the promise of a person with
> a clean heart will stay firm
> even till the end of time.'

'And further,

> It is the courageous ones who know
> what it means to say or do something;
> they will not resile, my child,
> from what they do or say.'

The merchant sent the old woman with his son to Suvarnadvipa without delay. All the citizens there were happy to see the young man again. Kalávati was most cordial, invited him courteously, and entertained him so well that he was soon eating out of her hand. She also relieved him once again of all his money. The question now is: what should the procuress Dhúrtamáyá do?

'I do not know!' said Prabhávati. 'You tell me, parrot.'

'All right,' the bird replied, 'I will tell you if you do not go out tonight.'

'I will not go,' she agreed, and the parrot continued the story.

Dhúrtamáyá dressed herself like an outcaste, and seemed always to be searching for something since some time before the courtesan took away Rama's money. One day she saw him sitting on the bed with Kalávati. He too saw her at the door and, as had already been arranged between them, he jumped up suddenly, as if to attack the procuress. Seeing him in this state, Kalávati also got up. 'What has happened?' she cried.

'Good woman,' Rama told the courtesan as he stood at the door as previously arranged, 'this is my mother. I stole her money, and she has not seen me for long.' Meanwhile Dhúrtamáyá was beckoning him with her hand. 'You have been caught after a long time, sir!' she screamed. 'So, you have been in the house of a prostitute! And you stole all my money for this vile whore!'

As she came cursing into the courtyard of the house, Rama too acted the outcaste and fell at her feet. Seeing this Kalávati and her keeper took the procuress inside. 'Mother,' they asked, 'who is he? What is his caste? Who are you?'

'I am Mátangi,' Dhúrtamáyá replied, 'the singer at the court of King Sudarshan, the lord of the city of Padmávati. This boy has come here after stealing my money, and I know that you have taken it. Now he must come with me to the king.'

Kalávati and her keeper grasped Dhúrtamáyá's feet. 'Take this money,' they pleaded. 'I will not take it here,' she replied. 'Not in the privacy of this house. I will take it after informing the king.'

The courtesan's mother was terrified. 'This is my daughter,' she told Dhúrtamáyá, 'please protect her. Take all the wealth we have accumulated through generations, but do not expose us to such humiliation.'

'I agree,' said Dhúrtamáyá, and the courtesan and her mother waited on her hand and foot. The procuress then retrieved her own money and took all of theirs too. Boarding a ship with Rama, she returned home and held a great festival there.

Prabhávati retired to sleep after listening to this story.

Here ends the twenty-third tale of Shuka Saptati

24

Sajjani's Presence of Mind

Prabhávati questioned the parrot once again on the following day. 'Go, madam,' said the bird, 'if you know what to say as did Sajjani to her husband when he caught her by the hair while she was with her paramour.'

There was a prosperous carpenter named Soorpál who lived in the town of Chandrapur. His wife Sajjani was exceedingly lustful of other men, and used to sleep with a person called Devak who lodged in their house.

Having learnt about this affair from others, the carpenter left his home one morning on the pretext of going out and, returning secretly at dusk, hid himself under the bed. As his wife was getting into it with her lover, he caught hold of her hair which hung below.

How will Sajjani extricate herself? The answer is that when her husband caught her out, she looked at her lover's face and said: 'I told you that my husband the carpenter is not at home.

It is only when he returns that he will take the proper decision about you. Though he did steal your money in the past, that should now be forgiven. I will come to your place when he returns, or I will get you both to meet together. There should be no doubt about this.'

Prabhávati went to bed after listening to this story.

Here ends the twenty-fourth tale of Shuka Saptati

25

Tale of the Two Sádhus

The next day Prabhávati once more asked the parrot about her going on a tryst. 'Do as you please,' the bird replied, 'if you know how to react like the white-robed monk when he was framed.'

In the city of Chandrapuri there used to be a Kshapanaka, a sádhu who goes about naked, named Siddhasen, who was much respected by the people. To the same city there came a Shvetámbara, that is, a monk who always wears a white habit. The new arrival was extremely competent, and all the people were attracted to him. He brought even the Buddhist votaries under his influence.

The naked sadhu was unable to tolerate the respect accorded to the white-robed one. He sent a prostitute to the latter's hermitage and spread the rumour that this monk was of bad character and lusted after harlots. He called on people to see the new arrival, saying 'the Kshapanaka alone is the true celibate and the Shvetámbara is a debauch.'

The white-robed sádhu on his part, set fire to his residence with the flame of a lamp as dawn was breaking. Stripping himself naked, he came out holding the prostitute's hand, so that the word spread that this was the nude Kshapanaka who was whoring, and not the Shvetámbara at all.

Prabhávati went to bed after listening to this story.

Here ends the twenty-fifth tale of Shuka Saptati

26

Ratna Devi and Her Two Lovers

⌇⌇⌇

'Go, madam!' said the parrot as Prabhávati was about to leave the next day. 'You will not be blamed if you know what to say like Ratna Devi did when her husband found her with two lovers.'

Ratna Devi was the wife of Kshemaraj, a brave kshatriya who lived in the village of Jalaud. The village head was one Devasákhya, who had a son named Dhaval. Both were Ratna Devi's lovers, though neither knew about the other. One day both father and son happened to be in her house when the kshatriya arrived. Now, what should be done?

On a signal from the woman, the village head marched out of the house, gesticulating with his finger as if to threaten someone. The kshatriya was scared. 'What has happened?' he asked his wife, as the other man went out.

'His son had sought refuge in your house,' Ratna Devi said with a laugh. 'But I did not surrender him to the father. For,

The kshatriya is one who guards good people,[1]
as the bow is an object for use as a weapon;
if neither does what they are meant to do,
the words themselves are meaningless.

'That is why the father went out so angrily. Now you can go
and escort the son back.' And this is what her husband did.

After listening to this story, Prabhávati retired to sleep.

Here ends the twenty-sixth tale of Shuka Saptati

27

The Thong

On the following day Prabhávati once more asked the parrot about her going for a rendezvous. 'Lovely legs,' the bird replied, 'who can stop someone driven by Káma? Go, mistress, if you can use your brains like Mohini.'

Now, Mohini was the wife of the merchant Arya who lived in the town of Shankhapur. A rogue named Kumukh would make love with her whenever she went out, and this was known to her husband. But he was an extremely timid man, and all he did was to stay by her side and prevent her from going out.

One day Mohini told the rogue: 'I will be in my husband's bed at night, but I will sleep behind him. Come there and make love with me.'

The lover did just that, but as he was doing it, the husband caught hold of the sign of his manhood. Now, how would the lover flee?

'Bring me a light,' the merchant told his wife, 'I have caught a thief.'

'I am afraid to go out,' said Mohini, 'I will hold him. You get the lamp.'

The merchant acted accordingly; meanwhile Mohini let the lover escape. She then took the thong from the leash of the dog tied inside the house, and lay down holding it as her husband came back with a lamp and a cudgel in his hands. 'Is this the thong from the dog's leash?' he asked. 'What is it doing here?'

'The dog was famished,' said Mohini. 'It was licking this thong and wore it out. Then it dropped this thing here.'

The merchant was silenced by this answer. 'You wretch!' his wife berated him, 'Such manly actions will be the end of you!' And, greatly ashamed, he went to sleep.

Prabhávati went to bed after listening to this story.

Here ends the twenty-seventh tale of Shuka Saptati

28

Devika Convinces Her Husband

'Slim waisted one,' replied the parrot when asked by Prabhávati the next day, 'go out this evening if you know what to say like Devika did in the past while she was with her lover.'

In the big village of Kuhad there lived a householder named Jaras who was a mighty fool. His wife Devika was an adulteress. A brahmin called Prabhakar would merrily make love to her in a quiet place by a plum tree in the middle of a field.

Jaras heard about this occurrence from other people, and went to the field to see it for himself. He climbed up the tree and saw exactly what he had been told. 'You minx!' he cried out while still sitting on his perch, 'today I have at last caught you after a long time!'

'Now then,' asked the parrot, 'how should she convince her husband?'

'I do not know!' said Prabhávati. 'Tell me yourself!'

'I will tell you if you do not go out,' said the parrot, and when she promised this, the bird continued.

'O my lord!' exclaimed Devika, 'this tree is bewitched! Whoever climbs it sees some lovemaking in progress.'

'All right,' said her husband. 'You climb and see.' And, going up the tree, she said wickedly: 'After a long time I see you lying with another woman.'

'This must be true!' the fool then concluded, and he pacified his wife and took her home.

Prabhávati went to sleep after listening to this story.

Here ends the twenty-eighth tale of Shuka Saptati

29

Sundari and the Spectre

'Go, dear madam,' said the parrot on Prabhávati's enquiry the next day, 'if you know how to apply your mind like Sundari who was caught at home with a lover.'

Sundari was the wife of the merchant Mahádhan who lived in the village of Sihuli. She had a lover named Mohan who was in the habit of coming to her house to sleep with her. Once, while she was thus occupied, her husband happened to return home. Now, what should she do?

The answer is that when she saw her husband coming, she got her lover to climb into a hammock on the wall, naked as he was. As for herself, she came out of the house with her hair undone and called out to her spouse from a distance: 'There is a naked ghostly figure sitting on the hammock in our house! Go and call the exorcists!'

While the fool Mahádhan went off to find an exorcist, Sundari took a lighted torch in her hand and got her paramour out of the house. 'The spectre vanished on seeing the fire,' she told her husband on his return.

Prabhávati retired to sleep after listening to this story.

Here ends the twenty-ninth tale of Shuka Saptati

30

A Ghoulish Choice

Questioned by Prabhávati on the following day, the parrot said: 'Go, my lady. I am not against your going if you know like Muladev[1] what to say in a crisis.'

There is in this land a cemetery called The Place of Ghosts. Two ghouls named Karál or Dreadful and Uttál or Frightful lived there with their wives Dhúmaprabhá or Smoky and Meghaprabhá or Cloudy. Once they had an argument about whose wife was more beautiful. At that time they and their wives chanced to see the rogue Muladev.

'Which among these two is more beautiful?' the ghouls asked Muladev, catching him in their arms. 'We will kill you if you lie.' Both their spouses were ancient she-ghouls, hideous and horrible to look at. If he stated the facts, he would be devoured. So, what should he say?

'The loveliest person in this world is no other than one's own beloved,' said that king of rogues. And the two ghouls let him go that very moment.

Prabhávati fell asleep after listening to this story.

Here ends the thirtieth tale of Shuka Saptati

31

The Lion and the Rabbit

Asked by Prabhávati the next day, the parrot said: 'Go and enjoy yourself as you please, good lady, if you have the rabbit's intelligence to help you in time of need.'

There was a lion named Pingala or Tawny in the forest of Madhura. He would kill many animals every day and, to put an end to this, all of them arranged to send one creature to him daily.

Once it came to be the rabbit's turn, but he would not move. 'Go,' said the animals, 'otherwise the lion will devour all of us as he used to do earlier.'

'No animal will go to him from now,' the rabbit observed, and he kept delaying his departure. It was only in the afternoon that he proceeded very slowly to present himself before the lion, who grabbed him in a trice. Now, how should he free himself? Here is the answer.

'Master,' the rabbit said to the lion, 'I was coming to you with four other rabbits, but your adversary caught us on the way. This is why I am late.'

'Where is that adversary?' the lion demanded.

The wily rabbit then took Pingala to an orchard and showed him his reflection in a well located there. Incensed at seeing the image, the foolish lion leapt into the water and perished.

> Intelligence, not prowess, lady,
> is what makes a creature strong;
> the mighty lion was despatched,
> behold, by just a rabbit.

It is said,

> The arrow discharged by the archer
> may or may not kill a man;
> but the ministers can most certainly
> destroy the king, state and people.

Prabhávati retired to sleep after reflecting over this story.

Here ends the thirty-first tale of Shuka Saptati

32

Rájini's Reply

O n the following day Prabhávati asked the parrot once again as she was about to leave. 'Go where you wish to, my lady of the lotus-face,' said the bird, 'if you know how to speak like Rájini did in the matter of substituting wheat with dust.'

In the town of Shantipur there lived a merchant called Madhav with his wife Mohini. They had a son named Sohad, whose wife Rájini was beautiful and clever as well as adulterous.

Once Rájini's mother-in-law gave her a silver dramma[1] coin and told her to go to the market and get some wheat. Rájini proceeded to the bazaar but, while she was making a purchase, she saw her lover there. She beckoned to him and, when he came up to her, she went off with him after tying the wheat in a bundle and leaving it in the market.

The grocer on his part removed the wheat from the bundle and tied some dust in it instead. Rájini spent a long time with her lover, and was in a hurry when she returned; so she took the bundle home without opening it again.

When the mother-in-law opened the bundle to see the wheat, all that she saw was the dust. 'What is this?' she asked, and what should the answer be?

'Mother,' said Rájini, 'the dramma fell out of my hand on the ground just in front of the market. That is why I have brought all the dust from there.' The older woman then inspected the dust, but was disappointed not to find the coin in it.

Prabhávati eventually fell asleep after listening to this story.

Here ends the thirty-second tale of Shuka Saptati

33

The Four Lovers of Rambhika

Prabhávati remained eager to go. Questioned by her the next day, the parrot said: 'What is the harm, my lady? Go, if you are able to act in a crisis like the flower-girl Rambhika did when her husband arrived.'

'How did that happen?' asked Prabhávati, and this is what the parrot recounted.

In the city of Shankhapur there lived a prosperous gardener named Shankar. His beautiful wife Rambhika was addicted to making love and, apart from being the favourite of her husband, also had many lovers.

Once the ceremony for the ancestors was to be observed in Shankar's house. Rambhika went out that day to sell flowers in the city square, and extended invitations to four of her lovers who were: a village headman, a merchant's son, a bodyguard and the chief of police. 'Come early to my house,' she told each of them separately, and none of them knew that the others too were invited.

On the following day, after Shankar had left for his garden, the merchant's son arrived with the intention of making love to Rambhika after bathing and eating at her house. He was only halfway through his bath when the village headman was seen at the door. Still bathing, the frightened merchant was bundled by Rambhika into a bamboo bin for storing grain which was full of discarded oilseed shells.

The village head was also in the bath when the bodyguard arrived. He too was pushed into the storage bin. 'A mother snake has laid eggs underneath,' he was told, 'so just stay inside.'

The bodyguard was still bathing when he was marched into the cupboard for utensils as the police chief had arrived. And the latter was sent half-bathed into the same place when the gardener returned home.

The gardener gave a lavish feast for a large number of people to mark the ceremony for his ancestors. The four lovers too were fed sumptuously without any of them knowing about the other.

The merchant's son ate noisily, and the village head sitting above him thought that the sounds came from the serpent below. He was so frightened that he pissed and the merchant, thinking that it was ghee, threw up his plate which struck the man above on his face. Even more frightened, the village head then jumped out, crying 'I have been struck! I have been struck!' The others were also terrified at his cries and bustled out as Shankar and his guests laughed with astonishment.

What will happen to Rambhika? The answer is that when her husband asked 'What is this?' she said: 'My dear, you have performed the commemorative ceremony without due faith! So your famished ancestors have come out without eating!' So the gardener had to perform the ritual all over again, while at Rambhika's instance her lovers escaped.

Once again Prabhávati retired to sleep after listening to this story.

Here ends the thirty-third tale of Shuka Saptati

34

How Shambhu Reclaimed the Sari

On the following day Prabhávati asked the parrot as usual about going out. 'Go, my lady,' the bird replied, 'if you know how to speak with guile like Shambhu, who gave the sari to the virgin in earlier times.'

'What is this story?' Prabhávati enquired, and this is what the parrot related.

In earlier times there was a brahmin named Shambhu who lived in a certain city. A professional gambler, he was given to roaming about in various countries.

Once, when he was on the road, he saw a pretty young girl guarding a field. After presenting her with a betel leaf roll and gaining her confidence with pleasant words, he asked her to sleep with him. 'You can take this sari I have,' he said, 'and let us make love.'

The girl complied with pleasure. But once the deed was done, the brahmin wanted the sari back. How should he get it?

The answer follows. When he asked her to give the sari back, the girl started going home. He followed her, holding five ears of corn in his hand. When they came to the village, he started screaming: 'O village elders! Look at this! There is something very strange in this village. For five ears of grain this girl has taken away my garment.'

The girl was too embarrassed to say anything, and the villagers made her give the sari back to Shambhu.

After listening to this story Prabhávati went away to sleep.

Here ends the thirty-fourth tale of Shuka Saptati

35

How Shambak Got Back His Ring

A sked the next day by Prabhávati, who was all dressed up to go for a rendezvous, the parrot said: 'Madam, there is no harm in going if, once you are there, you know how to get what you want like the buyer of sesame seeds.'

Once upon a time, in a certain village there was a merchant named Shambak who was a buyer of sesame seeds. He went to the village of Sargram where he visited the house of another merchant, a seller of utensils. This man was not at home, but his wife was, and she was not chaste. She and Shambak exchanged glances and promptly fell for each other. He gave her his ring and had her there and then. But, after their liaison, he wanted that ring back. The question is: how could he secure the return of a ring given away in these circumstances?

Unable to get the ring back, Shambak the sesame buyer confronted the seller of utensils in the marketplace. 'Give me the hundred measures of sesame for which I have already paid an advance,' he said.

'What sesame?' said the other merchant, 'and what advance? And who are you to speak like this?'

'Your wife has taken my ring as an advance for doubling the quantity of sesame,' claimed Shambak.

The utensil seller was enraged, and despatched his son to his wife. 'Our house will indeed prosper,' he had her told, 'if you carry on like this!'

The son came back with the ring and handed it over to the sesame buyer, who went back just as he had come. 'If you too have such intelligence,' said the parrot, 'then go by all means, Prabhávati but not otherwise.' And she retired to sleep after listening to this story.

Here ends the thirty-fifth tale of Shuka Saptati

36

The Tactfulness of Náyini

'I will go out, O parrot, and enjoy the pleasures I have long desired,' Prabhávati again told the bird the next evening. 'Pleasures must certainly be enjoyed,' the bird replied, 'that is the one certainty in this world. But you should know how to give answers like Náyini.'

'What is this story?' asked Prabhávati. 'Who was Náyini, parrot? Where did she give an answer, and what was it? Tell me this tale. It sounds auspicious and I am curious to know about it.' And this is what the parrot recounted.

Shoorapál was the headman of a village called Sarad. Náyini was his wife. She was always asking her husband to get her a bodice made of silk.

'We are farmers,' he told her. 'We wear cotton. In our homes no one even knows what is silk.'

One day Náyini called out to her husband while he was at the village assembly: 'Come home, master of the house! Come and eat your rávadi!'

Now rávadi is the pauper's food. Shoorapál came home on hearing his wife. 'Good woman,' he said to her, 'why did you utter such a deplorable and embarrassing word which did me no good in the assembly?'

'Why didn't you do what I wanted?' she shot back.

'I will get you the bodice today,' replied the headman, 'but you must counteract what you have said.'

'I will do that when you give me the bodice,' she said, and Shoorapál brought one for her. The question now is: how will her earlier words be countered?

The next day Náyini told her husband: 'When I call you today from the assembly hall as I did last time, you must come home with all the members.' He did that, and she gave a fine feast to the assembly members at her home. 'Shoorapál is a man of means,' the villagers said, 'and if his wife speaks like that, it is only to avoid sounding arrogant.' Thus did Náyini counteract her previous words with great finesse.

Prabhávati went to bed after listening to this story.

Here ends the thirty-sixth tale of Shuka Saptati

37

The Ploughman's Response

'Go as you please, good lady,' said the parrot on the following day, when Prabhávati questioned the bird. 'You will not at all be at fault if you know how to respond like the ploughman.'

Shoor was a landed farmer in the village of Sangam. He had a ploughman named Purnapal, upon whom he relied for everything: in the field, in the barn as well as in the house.

Shoor's daughter Subhaga would always take food for the ploughman when he was in the field and, without the least fear of his employer, he would make love to her in a nearby cave. Ploughmen from neighbouring fields considered this most unbecoming behaviour and informed Shoor about it.

Shoor went to the field on the following day to verify for himself the reported liaison between his daughter and the ploughman. Hiding near the cave, he beheld the couple engaged in intercourse. Now what will happen, and what is the solution? This is the question.

As the ploughman was getting up after making love to Subhaga, he spotted Master Shoor. 'Alas!' he said with a sigh, 'such is my karma that I am ordained to plough the field and she is sick with the wind. Perish us both. I am destined both to ply the plough and also to massage her stomach to draw out the wind. For what have I become Farmer Shoor's ploughman? It will be the end of me!'

After listening to these words Master Shoor concluded that what the others had said was false and the ploughman was innocent. Feeling greatly embarrassed, he went home.

As for Prabhávati, she retired to sleep after listening to the parrot's story.

Here ends the thirty-seventh tale of Shuka Saptati

38

The Brahmin's Ring

On the following night Prabhávati once more asked the parrot about her going out on a tryst. 'Nothing can stop people who are intent on doing what they want,' said the bird, 'but you should know how to do it like the brahmin Priyamvad.'

'What is this story?' Prabhávati demanded, and this is what the parrot recounted.

In days gone by, madam, there once a brahmin named Priyamvad, who was a traveller. While on his travels, he once arrived at the village of Sudarshan where he went to some merchant's house. The merchant's wife was a vamp, and seeing her the brahmin concluded that he had found a good place to stay. That night he propositioned her passionately and, while the merchant had gone to the market, he gave her a ring and took her to bed.

The next morning the brahmin asked for his ring, but the merchant's wife would not return it. The question is: how was he to get back a gift given in such circumstances; and here is the answer.

When the merchant's wife did not respond to Priyamvad's request, he picked up one of the bed posts and went to the merchant, weeping and displaying the wooden piece.

'What has happened, brahmin?' the merchant asked. 'The bed broke,' Priyamvad replied, 'and your wife took away my ring!'

The merchant was annoyed on hearing this. 'No traveller will ever come to our house if you make such mistakes,' he said to his wife harshly, and taking out the ring from the pit where she had buried it, he returned it to the brahmin who carried on with his travels.

After listening to this story Prabhávati retired to sleep.

Here ends the thirty-eighth tale of Shuka Saptati

39

Bhoodhar and the Balance

The next evening Prabhávati again asked the parrot about going to a paramour. 'I am leaving, parrot,' she said. 'Proceed, my lady,' replied the bird. 'Your going out to enjoy some handsome and fortunate man is an excellent idea if you know what to say in a crisis like the merchant with the balance.'

'Pray, what is this story, parrot?' Prabhávati asked. 'Who was the man with the balance? Where did he get it from, and what crisis did he confront? Tell me this interesting tale.' And this is what the parrot narrated.

There was a merchant named Bhoodhar in the town of Kundin. As his store of holy merit depleted,[1] so did his money. People began to avoid him. It is said,

> The rich man is wise,
> he is generous and good,
> the honoured kin of everyone;
> but when his money goes,
> so does his glory.

At last Bhoodhar was left with only an iron balance. Leaving it at the house of another merchant, he then proceeded abroad.

After earning wealth in other lands, Bhoodhar returned to his home town and asked the other merchant to return his balance. But the latter was not inclined to give it back. Covetous of the implement, and foolish too, he said in reply: 'Your balance has been eaten up by rats!'

Bhoodhar stayed silent on receiving such a reply. One day he went for a meal to the other merchant's house, and saw the latter's son playing outside. Secretly enticing the little boy, he carried him away to his own home.

The child's father and his family were grief stricken. Seeing them in tears, the neighbours said: 'O your son has been taken away by Bhoodhar.' So they went to his house and asked him for the boy.

'Friend,' replied Bhoodhar, 'your son had gone bathing in the river with me. But he was picked up there by an eagle and carried away!'

The other merchant went to the royal court and complained about his son's abduction. The question now is: how will the child's abductor extricate himself?

Questioned by the ministers before the king, Bhoodhar said: 'Sire, when rats can eat a balance made of iron, an eagle can carry off an elephant. It is not surprising that the same happened with a child.'

'When this rogue returns your balance,' said the minister after hearing Bhoodhar, 'only then should you restore the boy to him.' The other merchant was punished and made to surrender the balance while Bhoodhar returned the child.

Prabhávati retired to sleep after listening to this story.

Here ends the thirty-ninth tale of Shuka Saptati

40

Subuddhi and Kubuddhi

The next day, when Prabhávati asked the parrot about her going on a tryst, the bird replied: 'For those who really want to go, it is better that they go. So, carry on if, like Subuddhi, you know what should or should not be said.'

'What is this story?' asked Prabhávati, and this is what the parrot recounted.

Subuddhi and Kubuddhi were well known as a friendly couple among the people in the city of Nagar. Once Subuddhi went to another country, and Kubuddhi became intimate with his wife. In due course Subuddhi returned from abroad after earning much wealth. Kubuddhi then put on a false display of affection for his friend, who also treated the other man with respect.

'Sir, did you see anything marvellous anywhere?' Kubuddhi asked the friend who had just returned.

'I saw an unseasonal mango fruit floating in a well in the village of Manoram on the banks of the river Sarasvati,' replied Subuddhi.

'That is a lie,' retorted Kubuddhi.

'It is true,' Subuddhi insisted.

'If it turns out to be true,' said Kubuddhi, 'then you can take from my house whatever you can hold in your two hands. If not, I will do the same from your house.'

Having made this wager, Kubuddhi brought out the fruit from the well at night. In its absence Subuddhi lost the bet. Kubuddhi, who desired his friend's wife, then demanded that the condition of the wager be fulfilled.

The question here is: what should Subuddhi do to safeguard his spouse? The answer was given by the parrot.

Aware of Kubuddhi's evil intentions, Subuddhi placed his wife, together with all his domestic goods, upon the roof of his house and put the ladder on the ground.

Kubuddhi arrived. 'Take from our house whatever pleases you,' said Subuddhi. As his friend then took hold of the ladder with both his hands in order to get to his wife, Subuddhi interjected: 'I have already told you that you can take whatever you hold in your two hands, and nothing else!'

Ashamed and abashed, Kubuddhi slunk away, while the people mocked and ridiculed him.

After listening to this story, Prabhávati went away to sleep.

Here ends the fortieth tale of Shuka Saptati

41

The Incantation of Spring

'I will go if you agree, parrot,' said the merchant's bride on the following day. 'My lady,' the bird replied, 'it will be appropriate for you to go if, on getting there, you know something to say in a crisis, like the brahmin.'

There was a king named Shatrumardan in the city of Panchapur. His daughter developed a goitre in the neck, and the physicians gave it up as incurable.

The king made a proclamation with the beating of the drum, that he would give great wealth to whoever cured his daughter Madanarekhá. A brahmin's wife, who had come from some village, heard the proclamation and put her hand on the drum.[1] 'My husband is adept in incantations,' she said on being questioned, 'he will be able to cure the princess.'

As the king's men were taking the brahmin to the court, his wife told him: 'Lord, go to the city. Curing the princess will get you great gain.' But he knew no incantations or any

such thing. The question is: what will happen once he is seated
in the ritual circle? The parrot gave an answer.

The so-called incantationist occupied the ceremonial seat
and commenced a recitation:

> The worth of living, I well know,
> why renounce and spoil it so?
> Rest at home, O brahmin's wife
> and serve your spouse for a happy life.

> The forest smiles, the buds are gleaming,
> it shines with mango blossoms teeming.
> Here rows of milk trees, branches bent
> with loads of fruit, so succulent;
> there rose apple and timburini
> in splendid clusters one may see.
> Here serried oleanders shine,
> there camphor spreads its fragrance fine.
> Here jasmine fair and pepper vine,
> there mango, sandalwood and pine,
> champak, bakula, pomegranate flowers,
> palm and jujube trees in bowers
> by nets of climbing gourd entwined
> so thick—the sky one cannot find.
> The fruit is red on the karna plant,
> others the jungle white rose flaunt;
> some are covered by the wild anise,
> and flowers bloom on sindur trees

in festoons which entrance the mind
with their glory, incarnadined.
In blossom too are coral trees,
high acacias scent the breeze;
and other plants with blooms are dense,
double jasmine charms the sense.[2]

As the brahmin recited these verses, the princess began to laugh. She laughed so much that the goitre on her neck burst, and she was cured. The king duly rewarded the brahmin who returned to his home.

Prabhávati went to sleep after listening to this story.

Here ends the forty-first tale of Shuka Saptati

42

The Tiger Slayer

'I am going,' Prabhávati told the parrot the following day. 'Enjoyment of pleasure is the best thing in this world,' the bird replied. 'Go, my beauty, if you know how to respond like the tiger slayer.'

'Enjoyment of pleasure?' asked Prabhávati. 'Tell me the story, parrot.' And the parrot told her the following tale.

In the village of Devul there lived a man named Raj Singh of the warrior caste. His wife was notorious as a shrew. Once she had a fight with her husband and, taking her two sons, set off for her father's house. Full of anger, she went through many towns and woodlands, and came at last to a great forest by the side of the Malaya mountains.

What was this forest like? It bristled with sandalwood and devil trees, under a canopy of the branches of tall pines. Here and there were mango, date and jackfruit trees, swarming with intoxicated bees and birds. Some parts of the interior were full of palm and cordia; others were thick with succulent jujube and tamarind. The fragrance of the pomegranate and the woodapple filled the forest air.

Proceeding inside this dense forest, the shrew beheld a tiger who also saw her and her sons. The beast struck the ground with its tail and charged at them. Now what will happen? That is the question.

The parrot gave the answer. Seeing the tiger approach, the shrew brazenly slapped her two sons, saying: 'Why do you two quarrel about eating one tiger each? Eat this one after dividing it. We may see another one later.'

The tiger overheard the shrew. 'This woman must be the tiger slayer,' it concluded and, frightened out of its wits, promptly ran away.

'Dear girl,' said the parrot, 'that woman saved herself from the tiger by her own intelligence. Similarly do other clever people also counter great dangers in this world.'

Prabhávati went to sleep after listening to this story.

Here ends the forty-second tale of Shuka Saptati

43

The Tiger Slayer-II

'Proceed, my lady of the majestic gait,' said the parrot when that charming woman asked it again the next day, 'it is not at all improper for you to go if you can keep your wits about you as did the tiger slayer on the second occasion.'

'What now is this story, you sweet talker?' Prabhávati enquired. 'Tell me about the tiger slayer's second display of intelligence. I am full of curiosity.'

'The wiliest among the animals of the forest is the jackal,' the parrot related. Seeing the terrified tiger in flight, it said with a laugh: 'Why are you running away so scared, tiger?'

'Flee, jackal!' cried the tiger. 'You too should get away to some secret place. I was on the verge of being killed by the tiger slayer woman about whom we hear in the scriptures. I ran away from her and just about escaped with my life.'

'Tiger!' exclaimed the cunning creature, 'what you say is astonishing! You are scared of that lump of flesh, a mere human?'

'I saw her with my own eyes!' said the tiger. 'She slapped both her sons who were quarrelling, as each of them wanted to devour me!'

'Let us go and find that rogue of a woman, master,' the jackal said. 'When we get there, I pledge you my life if she as much as looks at you.'

'What will your pledge be worth, jackal?' the tiger retorted, 'if you abandon me and go off.'

'In that case tie me to your neck,' said the jackal. 'But let us go quickly.'

The tiger returned to the forest after doing what the jackal had advised. The tiger slayer woman was already there with her sons. The question is: how will she save herself from the tiger, now incited by the jackal?

'The tiger has been brought here by that other crafty animal,' the woman said to herself. Then, scolding the jackal and wagging her finger at it in a threatening manner, she cried: 'You scoundrel! Earlier you gave me three tigers. Today you have brought only one! How can you go away now? Tell me!' Then she rushed forward to frighten them, and the tiger suddenly turned tail and fled, the jackal still tied to its neck.

'Thus did that woman save herself once again by her intelligence from the danger posed by the tiger,' the parrot said in conclusion. 'Intelligence, my lady, prevails in all things at all times.'

And, after listening to this story, Prabhávati went to sleep.

Here ends the forty-third tale of Shuka Saptati

44

The Tiger Slayer-III

Asked by Prabhávati on the following evening, the parrot said: 'Go, madam, if like the jackal you know how to protect yourself in an emergency.'

The tiger was frightened of the killer-woman, and wanted to run away to some other land. The jackal was dragged along as it was tied by the neck to the tiger. Its back and feet badly scraped, blood flowing from its throat, the jackal was almost dead by now. The question is: how may it save itself in this grave emergency? The parrot gave the answer.

The tiger fled at great speed, crossing many rivers and woods, through even and uneven terrain and hills. Observing its headlong progress, and eager to free itself, the jackal laughed out loud, even though it was in pain.

'Why are you laughing?' the tiger asked.

'Sire,' replied the jackal, 'I had thought that tiger slayer to be just a charlatan. By your grace I am now far away from her and still alive. But how will we survive if that witch comes after us, following the stains left by my blood drops? That is why I laughed. We must stop and think about this, my lord.'

'That's right,' said the tiger, looking pleased at the jackal's remark. And, suddenly detaching itself from the other animal, it continued in flight. As for the jackal, it was relieved to stay back.

'For those who want wealth, fame and happiness, the best means is intelligence,' said the parrot. 'Those without intelligence only suffer miseries, my beauty.'

> The strength of the witless
> only serves others:
> we see this in the elephant
> tall as a mountain.

After listening to this story, Prabhávati retired to sleep, marvelling at the parrot's words.

Here ends the forty-fourth tale of Shuka Saptati

45

The Worsting of Vishnu

'I will go!' that charming girl declared to the parrot the next day, in the evening.

'The present is a proper time for you to have a lover, my dear,' the parrot replied, 'if you know, like Vishnu of old, how to do something in case of being cheated.'

'What is this story?' Prabhávati enquired, and this is what the parrot related.

In the city of Vilaspur, which was ruled by King Arindam, there lived a brahmin named Vishnu who had been forsaken by his family. He was a great lover, and it was well-known in the city that no woman could match him: what to say of ladies of good family, even harlots were unable to worst him in lovemaking.

Ratipriya was a courtesan in the same city. Having been paid a sum of sixteen silver drammas,[1] she invited Vishnu to her house, and welcomed him with flattering words on his arrival. He had finished his other work and his mind was already set on making love. So he commenced forthwith, intent on achieving a victory.

It may have been for the money, or because she wished to defeat him, but the courtesan endured that ardent lover for two full watches. At last she came down and told her procuress: 'This brahmin is insupportable. Return his money and get him out. What we already have will be more than enough, if I survive.'

'In our house no lover has ever outlasted a courtesan and got back the price,' said the procuress. 'So, put up with him till I devise a strategm to dislodge him. I will climb the peepal tree and crow like a cock, while making the sound of flapping wings with a couple of baskets for winnowing grain. You should then send him off, saying it is morning.' With these words the procuress sent the courtesan back upstairs.

The procuress acted as she said she would, and the brahmin was sent away on the grounds that day had dawned. When he came out and looked at the sky, it was still very much night. Now, having been worsted by the procuress, how will he explain this defeat before the people? That is the question.

Looking in the direction from where the cock's crows had emanated, the brahmin saw the procuress still sitting on the tree with the two winnowing baskets in her hands. Throwing stones at her, he brought her down and had her condemned by other women. He also took twice the amount of money he had paid, and derided the courtesan in the city before going home.

Prabhávati went off to sleep after listening to this story.

Here ends the forty-fifth tale of Shuka Saptati

46

The Brahmin and the Ghost

'Leave your house and go, madam,' said the parrot when Prabhávati questioned the bird next day, 'but only if you know what to say, as did the husband of Karagará, in dispelling the ghost.'

In the city of Vatsom, my lady, there lived a learned but poor brahmin with his beloved wife Karagará. In keeping with her name, she caused alarm and anxiety to every creature, so much so that the ghost who lived on the tree by her gate was frightened of her and fled to the forest. The brahmin too was affected by her and decided to go abroad.

The ghost saw the brahmin on his way. 'You must be tired of travelling,' it said to him, 'be my guest today.'

'Whatever hospitality you wish to provide,' the brahmin replied apprehensively, 'please offer it quickly.'

'Do not be afraid,' the ghost assured him. 'You are my master, for I am the ghost that lived on the tree by the gate of your house. I came here as I was scared of Karagará. Some service of quality must certainly be rendered to one's master, that is yourself. Therefore, brahmin, go to Mrigávati, the capital of King Madan. I will possess his daughter Mrigalochaná. No other exorcist will be able to cure her, but when you arrive I will abandon her merely at your sight. After that, however, you should not attempt any further exorcism.'

The ghost then proceeded to the royal capital, and possessed the princess. The brahmin went there too, and touched the drum beaten for the proclamation. Thereafter he was taken to the palace, where he made the necessary arrangements for the exorcism. But the ghost would not leave the princess, and the question is: what should the brahmin do?

Addressing the recalcitrant phantom, the brahmin said: 'You rogue of a ghost, I am the husband of Karagará. I came here in good faith. Abide by your promise, sir. Is it proper to deceive me? It is said,

> When people of good family,
> and monks observing celibacy,
> never utter falsehoods;
> then is it proper for celestials?'

The ghost then left the princess and departed. 'She is cured,' said the king, and gave half his kingdom as well as his daughter to the brahmin. The latter also went his way, all his wishes fulfilled.

Prabhávati retired to bed after listening to this story.

Here ends the forty-sixth tale of Shuka Saptati

47

The Brahmin and the Ghost-II

The day passed, and once again Prabhávati consulted the parrot about going to meet a lover. 'Go, my lady,' the bird replied, 'if you know what to say like Karagará's husband, when there was a crisis with the ghost.'

Karagará's husband enjoyed the kingdom together with the princess. Meanwhile, the ghost went to the city of Karnávati and took possession of Sulochana, the wife of King Shatrughna there. This lady was the paternal aunt of King Madan of Mrigávati. Suffering greatly in consequence of being possessed, she asked for an exorcist to be sent from her parents' kingdom.

The exorcist who was deputed happened to be Keshav, the husband of Karagará. He had no desire to go, but the king sent his messengers to persuade him with pleasant words and, on the insistence of his new wife, he went to Karnávati.

King Shatrughna received the brahmin with great respect and sent him to Queen Sulochana's palace. The ghost saw him coming, and threatened him with harsh words. 'I kept my promise in one place,' it said, 'now, brahmin, save yourself if you can.'

The question is: what will happen to the brahmin? He knew no incantations or other ritual, but he did understand what the occasion required. Realising that this was the same ghost that he had encountered earlier, he clasped his hands in supplication and whispered into the spectre's ear: 'Ghost, Karagará is now here! She followed me, her husband, to this place. That is what I have come to tell you!'

The ghost was astonished as well as terrified at hearing these words. 'I am going, brahmin,' it said, and promptly left the queen. Seeing her cured, Shatrughna duly honoured the brahmin who then returned to the city of Mrigávati.

Prabhávati went to bed after listening to this story.

Here ends the forty-seventh tale of Shuka Saptati

48

The Two Mares

'Should I go and take a lover?' Prabhávati asked the parrot the next day. 'Making love gives the best of pleasures in this world, my beauty,' said the bird. 'Go, if you know like Shakatál how to take a decision in an emergency.'

Once upon a time there was an emperor named Nanda in the city of Patalipura. Shakatál was his prime minister. All other rulers had been eclipsed by Shakatál's intellectual powers, and had become Nanda's tributaries. It is said,

> What is the worth of a servant, who[1]
> is loyal, but has no brains or courage?
> Equally, what is the benefit of one
> who is clever and brave, but lacks devotion?
> But those, in whom the qualities
> of valour, wit and loyalty

> are combined, truly are servants
> who further a king's prosperity
> in times of weal and woe.
> The rest are but concubines.

What is more,

> What can foes united do[2]
> to one by intelligence protected?
> Just like rainfall on a person
> when with an umbrella deflected.

The minister once restrained the king from acting in a manner which would have destroyed the law and despoiled the land. The foolish monarch had him confined within a dry well, where he and his sons remained for a long time. Meanwhile the word spread everywhere that Shakatál, the prime minister, was dead.

To investigate these reports, the lord of Bengal then sent his personal agents with a pair of mares to Nanda. The agents had been directed to return after ascertaining which of the two animals was the mother and which the daughter, in accordance with the signs determined by the equestrian authority Shalihotra.

No one in Nanda's kingdom was able to decide about the mares. 'I am being humiliated in the absence of Shakatál,' the king reflected. 'It is said

> As between the loss of territory,
> and of a wise, meritorious servant,
> the latter is like death for kings;
> for land is easily gained, not servants.'

Having thought this over, Nanda asked the officer charged with arrests and punishments if anyone from Shakatál's family was still alive in the well. 'Someone is still there,' the officer replied, 'for that person takes the cooked rice which is sent in. But I do not know personally who it is.'

The king had the prisoner taken out of the well with all honour. 'You are my friend, innocent one,' he said, 'my respected guru and guide, my executor and refuge. What are you not to me? It is said

> In what did you not help me?
> A guide in warding off mistakes,
> a guru in preaching the scriptures,
> a repository of secrets, a carrier out
> of orders, a refuge in times of fear;
> you gave me the seven sea girdled earth,
> you were my best friend in every way.'

'Command me, master,' said the minister, for it was Shakatál, 'what should I do?'

'Which is the mother and which the daughter, among these two mares?' said the king. 'You should quickly dispel this doubt raised by these cunning envoys.'

The question is: how should the minister lay this doubt at rest? He had the two mares saddled, and raced them in an open field. When they were tired out, he removed their harness and had them released, whereupon they began to act like mother and daughter. The mother licked the daughter with her tongue, the filly nuzzled the dam, and the wise minister explained the relationship between the two to the king. Thus did Shakatál win much wealth and praise.

Prabhávati went away to sleep after listening to this story.

Here ends the forty-eighth tale of Shuka Saptati

49

The Ring of Cane

The following day, having done her daily duties, Prabhávati questioned the parrot once again. 'My lady,' the bird replied, 'it will be in order for you to enjoy the pleasures of lovemaking today if you can act with skill in a crisis, as Shakatál did once again.'

As on the previous occasion, the lord of Bengal sent the same men with a ring of cane to ascertain if Shakatál was alive. 'Go to Nanda's kingdom,' he commanded them, 'and find out at which point this circle of cane commences, and where does it end.'

The messengers placed the cane ring, which was embellished with gold, diamonds and other gems, before Nanda, and asked where it began and ended. Leading connoisseurs and merchants weighed the cane and otherwise examined it, but none could discern its beginning or its end.

'Excepting you no one knows how this cane is constituted,' the king said to Shakatál. 'You alone can provide the answer.'

'Your supposition cannot remain groundless, master,' said Shakatál. 'It is held that

> One who lets his king's command
> stay in a crisis unfulfilled
> is like the blemish in the moon,
> though pure and noble he may be.'

Though the minister was expected to know the answer, how was he to find it? That is the question, and the wise premier made a judgement by placing the cane in water, when its root sank somewhat. He explained this to the monarch who conveyed it in turn to the messengers. They informed their own king, and he and the other rulers then resumed the payment of their tribute to Emperor Nanda.

Prabhávati retired to sleep after listening to this story.

Here ends the forty-ninth tale of Shuka Saptati

Dharmabuddhi and Dushtabuddhi

'Go, my lady,' replied the parrot when Prabhávati asked the bird the next day as she was preparing to leave. 'I see nothing wrong in your going if you know like Dharmabuddhi how to act in adversity.'

'What is this story?' she asked, and this is what the parrot said.

Dharmabuddhi and Dushtabuddhi were two friends who lived in a village called Jángal in this land. Once they went abroad in search of wealth and, having earned a great deal of money, returned after some time to their own village.

Consulting with each other at the time of their return, the two friends decided to bury a part of their wealth under a peepal tree, and take home the balance; the buried treasure, they agreed, could later be divided gradually as the need arose. Having done this, they went to their respective abodes where they lived happily, content and occupied with the enjoyment of pleasures.

Listen now to what Dushtabuddhi did meanwhile. It is not proper to talk about it, for

> One should never talk, my lady,
> of evils seen or heard about;
> for, it's clear, that even talking
> of evil causes problems enough.

What happened was that Dushtabuddhi dug out the treasure and took it away to his home.

In course of time the two men went together to retrieve the money buried under the peepal tree. They looked for it, but it was nowhere to be found. Dharmabuddhi then went to the magistrate and, after recounting the affair, accused Dushtabuddhi of having stolen the money. The latter, who had also been summoned, replied that he had left a thousand coins under the tree. 'I will invoke divine testimony for this,' he affirmed, and the magistrate agreed that this may be done. The plaintiff also having accepted this course, sureties were taken from both parties and they were permitted to go home. Meanwhile, Dushtabuddhi explained the situation to his own father and hid him in the hollow of the tree.

The next morning the magistrate went with both suitors and many curious onlookers to the peepal tree. Dushtabuddhi, freshly bathed, clasped his hands together and swore an oath.

'Best of trees,' he cried, 'speak truly. If the money was stolen by me, say so. If it was not, say that too.'

'It was not!' said Dushtabuddhi's father, addressing the assembled people from his hiding place. The question now is: what will happen to Dharmabuddhi?

Asked by Prabhávati the parrot continued the story. Realising that the voice from the tree was that of Dushtabuddhi's father, Dharmabuddhi set fire to the hollow of the tree. Soon his friend's parent fell out of it, screaming and half-burnt. After seeing this, the magistrate pronounced a punishment for Dushtabuddhi, and caused Dharmabuddhi to be compensated.

Prabhávati retired to sleep after listening to this story.

Here ends the fiftieth tale of Shuka Saptati

51

Gangil's Bluff

'You are greedy for the taste of love, O charming one,' said the parrot to the girl when she asked the bird on the following day. 'Go if you are aware of what to say when in trouble, like Gangil.'

'I do not know this,' said Prabhávati, 'tell me about it.' And the parrot related this story.

There is a city called Chamatkárapuri, which was full of people from all the four castes and stations of life who were adept in the four Vedas.

Once the brahmins of the city set forth on a pilgrimage to the shrine of the lord of Vallabhi. Full of enthusiasm, they travelled in carts and on horseback, and carried provisions for the journey. They were prosperous, well-dressed people, and were accompanied by their wives and children. On the road they were waylaid by bandits.

The frightened brahmins began to flee, but one of them was unable to do so as he was lame. Gangil by name, he stayed inside a cart and was soon surrounded. The question is: what will happen to him?

When the others had fled, the brahmin in the cart spoke out aloud to his agitated brother. 'How many elephants and horses are there outside, brother?' he shouted loudly, as if he were a brave warrior. 'Tell me quickly, and give me the bow so that I may destroy them all together with this divine missile.' Hearing his words, all the bandits also ran away.

> One who knows what to say
> in dharma, artha, and káma[1] too:
> which man can defeat him
> O lady with the lotus face?

After listening to this story, Prabhávati went off to sleep.

Here ends the fifty-first tale of Shuka Saptati

52

Jayashri and the Four Gems

The day was over. 'I am going,' Prabhávati said to the parrot as night descended. 'Go to your lover, my lady,' the bird replied, 'if you know like Jayashri what to do in your own interest.'

'What is this tale?' asked Prabhávati. 'Listen, my lady,' said the parrot, and recounted this story.

There is, upon this earth, a city called Pratishthan. The king there was Sattvasheel, and he had a son named Durdaman.

'I should not be living on my patrimony,' prince Durdaman once said to himself, 'but only on what I earn on my own.' Thinking thus, he quit the city and set off for another country with his like-minded friends, who were a brahmin, a carpenter and the son of a merchant.

The four friends put their heads together and concluded that they should render service to that repository of gems, the Ocean. As it is said,

For the learned and the well-born,
for those possessed of wealth and valour,
the proper place is with the king,
or one better even than that.

And,

Only the good can find solutions
to the problems of good people;
only elephants can support
other elephants caught in quicksand.

Having thought this over, they served the Ocean by keeping a fast for twenty-one days. The Ocean was satisfied and gave them four gems with the same qualities as the Chintámani, the famous wishing jewel.

The four friends turned back, gratified at having obtained the four gems, which the other three handed over in good faith to the merchant's son. But that villain was overcome by greed. He hid the precious stones inside his thigh, in an incision which he sewed up. Later on, he dropped behind on the road and started screaming and shouting: 'I have been robbed!'

'What happened?' asked the others. 'I had stayed behind to pass water,' said the merchant's son, 'and a thief stole everything I had.'

'This son of the merchant is a rogue,' the others reflected on hearing his explanation. 'He would definitely have committed some fraud.' Thinking and arguing about this, they proceeded to the city of Airavati.

The king of Airavati was the well-known Nitisára. His minister Buddhisára was famous the world over with the reputation that he could judge an actuality merely from the statements made by suitors. The prince and the others approached this minister and told him about the loss of their gems as it had occurred. 'Please find the gems,' they requested him, 'and without sentencing anyone to death or imprisonment, just distribute them between us, one for each. If you cannot ascertain and do this, your worldwide reputation is bound to be ruined.'

Buddhisára was stricken with worry on receiving this request. The question is: what will become of him and his king?

Unable to determine which of the four had the gems, the minister went home dejected. Now, he had a daughter named Jayashri who was in the flush of youth. She had meanwhile come to greet her father after praying to the goddess Párvati. Seeing him distraught, she asked him the reason for his distress, and he told her what had happened.

'Do not worry, father,' said Jayashri, 'I will judge between these men. When these suitors come for their judgement, send them home, and I will deliver to you the one who stole the gems.'

'Daughter!' said the minister, 'when I could not find this out, how will you do it?'

'You must not speak like that, father,' Jayashri replied. 'Minds are different in everyone. One expert knows one thing in this world, and another knows something else.

In every head is a different mind
and in each mouth a separate voice;
as every pond has distinct water,
and every home its own mistress.

Problems fly from men whose eyes
are illuminated with wisdom,
just as darkness flees before
the hand which holds the lamp.

'Therefore, father, do not worry at all. Just send these strangers here so that I may judge between them.'

The minister sent the four men to his daughter, who had them bathed, fed and lodged in separate rooms. She then ornamented herself and went first to the prince. 'I have come to you, looking for pleasure,' she said to him. 'Give me a hundred pieces of gold and sleep with me.'

'I will earn money, even a kingdom, and give it to you,' said he, 'but at present I have nothing at all.'

Seeing that the prince was penniless, Jayashri then went to the brahmin and told him exactly what she had said to his friend. 'My father has money and title to land,' the brahmin responded, 'I will give you all that.'

Knowing him to be destitute also, Jayashri left the brahmin and went to the carpenter who said: 'I have nothing at present, but I will give you a hundred thousand later.'

Abandoning the poor carpenter, the minister's daughter then went to the merchant's son and spoke to him similarly.

'Mistress!' he exclaimed, 'take these four gems, and make love to me!' And, extracting the gems from his thigh, he gave them to her there and then.

Making some excuse to get up and safeguard her maidenhood, Jayashri then returned to her own abode. She gave the four gems to her father who called each of the suitors and gave them their share.

They were delighted to regain their property and went back to their respective homes.

Prabhávati retired to sleep after listening to this story.

Here ends the fifty-second tale of Shuka Saptati

53

Ðevika Averts a Crisis

'My lady of the lovely legs,' said the parrot, when questioned by Prabhávati the next day, 'your going will be in order if you know what to do in a crisis like the wife of the leathersmith.'

There is a village called Charmakúta or Leather Hill on the banks of the river Charmanvati. A leathersmith named Dohad lived there with his wife Devika, who was extremely promiscuous. Once, when the leathersmith had gone out to purchase leather, she brought a lover home. As the couple finished making love, her husband appeared outside with the leather. Now, what will happen to her and her paramour? This is the question. Asked by Prabhávati, the parrot gave the following answer.

As soon as she realised that her husband had returned, Devika came outside, muttering meaningless words. The foolish leathersmith was scared, and rushed to the village to fetch an exorcist. Meanwhile she got her lover out and he went home.

'If you also know what to do in a crisis, then go,' said the parrot. 'Otherwise go to bed.' And Prabhávati retired to sleep.

Here ends the fifty-third tale of Shuka Saptati

54

The Ambassador's Presence of Mind

Once again Prabhávati asked the parrot, having passed the day longing to go out. 'Go, my lady,' the bird replied. 'What is the harm in going if you know how to speak like the ambassador did once when confronted with a crisis before the king?'

In the city of Shakrávati there was a king named Dharma Datta who was endowed with righteousness and all the other virtues. He had a minister, Sushil by name, whose son Vishnu had formerly been responsible for matters pertaining to war and peace. On removal from that post, the man had become impoverished, but remained haughty and proud that he had been a minister of the royal household. The king said nothing, but the minister Sushil once asked him: 'Why is Vishnu not granted any favour whatsoever?'

Being displeased with Vishnu, the king kept silent. The minister however persisted. 'This Vishnu is loyal and devoted to you, master,' he said. 'Besides he is an expert in diplomatic work. He should be sent somewhere by Your Majesty and put to a test.'

The king listened to the minister's words, but continued to disfavour his son. He sealed a parcel of ashes with his own seal and sent Vishnu with it to King Shatrudaman in the city of Vidisha.

Vishnu went to Vidisha and opened the sealed parcel before the king, unaware that its contents were ashes. The king was livid with rage at the presentation of such an inauspicious gift before him. How will the ambassador who brought the gift ensure his own welfare? That is the question to which the parrot provided the answer.

Seeing the king enraged, the wise Vishnu said: 'Your Majesty, my master has performed the horse sacrifice. He offers this pure, auspicious and sin-dispelling ash generated by the triple flame of the sacrificial fire pit to you for reverence. For, in his words,

> You and I possess, O king,
> elephants, horses, goods diverse;
> but holy, sacrificial ashes
> are extremely hard to find.'

And, getting up all of a sudden, he took the ashes in his hand and presented them to the king of Vidisha, who paid his respects to them, satisfied with Vishnu's words. The contented king also sent back a large reciprocal gift with Vishnu before dismissing him with all honour.

'You too, dear lady,' the parrot concluded, 'if you know how to deal with a crisis, then go. Otherwise stay at home.' And Prabhávati retired to sleep after listening to this story.

Here ends the fifty-fourth tale of Shuka Saptati

55

The Brahmin and the Shoemaker

The next night Prabhávati again questioned the parrot about going on a tryst. 'Go, lady of the lovely legs and the majestic gait,' the parrot replied, 'if you know how to give an answer like the brahmin Shridhar.'

'What is this story?' asked Prabhávati, and this is what the parrot related.

There was a brahmin named Shridhar in the village of Charmakúta. A shoemaker called Chandan lived in the same village, and Shridhar had a pair of shoes made by him.

The shoemaker was always asking for his money. 'I will make you happy,' the brahmin would reply, and much time passed in this way. One day the shoemaker caught hold of the brahmin. How can he escape without paying? This is the question, and here is the answer.

Meanwhile a son had been born in the village headman's house. The brahmin resorted to a trick and said: 'Shoemaker,

I had told you that I would make you happy. Now that this son has been born, are you happy or not?'

If the shoemaker said that he was not happy, he could face authority's ire; otherwise he would lose the money. In the circumstances he replied: 'I have been made very happy.'

'The brahmin went home after saving himself by a a trick in this way,' said the parrot. 'If you know how to give such an answer, then go, dear lady.' But Prabhávati retired to sleep after hearing this story.

Here ends the fifty-fifth tale of Shuka Saptati

56

The Merchant and the Bandits

On the following day Prabhávati asked the parrot once more about going out. 'Go, madam,' the bird replied, 'if you know how to deal with a difficult situation like Sántak the merchant did in times bygone.'

In the village of Tripath there lived an extremely rich merchant named Sántak. Miserly and bad-tempered, he preferred to do his business in other villages. Once he was returning home after collecting money he had loaned out in another village, when he was waylaid by bandits.

'The question, dear lady, is how will he free himself from this fearful situation,' said the parrot, 'and here is the answer.'

Realising that he had been caught by bandits, the merchant proceeded to the nearby temple of a yaksha[1] named Galagraha. He placed the money before the deity and, taking a crayon in his hand, he thus addressed the great yaksha: 'Lord, here's the money, inclusive of interest, that I have obtained after collecting from everyone the debts they owed to you.'

The bandits saw the merchant writing these words, and concluded that the money indeed appertained to the yaksha. They therefore saluted him and went away. As for Sántak, he took the cash and went home safely.

Prabhávati went away to sleep after listening to this story.

Here ends the fifty-sixth tale of Shuka Saptati

57

Thℯ King and thℯ Poℯt

'I am going,' the girl told the parrot the next evening. 'I will enjoy myself today, making love with another man.' 'Go, my lady,' replied the bird, 'if you know what to say should your husband learn about this, as did the wise Shubhankar in earlier times when the king came to know about his affair.'

At that time Vikramaditya was the king in the land of Avanti. He had a queen named Chandralekha who had become infatuated with the court poet Shubhankar. Changing clothes with a slave-girl, she would go to his house and make love with him as she pleased.

The affair between the queen and the poet had already been in progress for some time when the season of the rains arrived. King Monsoon comes with the crashing drum beat of thunder, the roaring music of the clouds and the conquering banner of crying peacocks. Dark days and slushy roads, torrents of rain and flashes of lightning, have always obstructed the meetings of lovers. It is said,

> If she loves me, she will die;
> if she lives, she loves me not;
> either way, my darling's lost:
> wicked cloud, why do you thunder?

Such was the season when the queen set off for Shubhankar's house one night. King Vikramaditya saw her go and became curious. Covered with a dark cloak, he followed her in secret, a sword in his hand.

As Shubhankar saw the queen arrive at his door, he recited:

> When thundering clouds have deepened darkness
> and all the quarters are obscured;
> when the air is filled with shouts
> of guards and watchful sentinels;
> at such a time, when like a flame
> emerging from the sea of his wrath,
> you come to me from the king's bedchamber:
> O lotus eyes, I then believe
> that women only pretend they are afraid.

The king returned to his palace after listening to the poet's recitation. As for Shubhankar, he gratified the queen with sweet words and various refinements of pleasure. It is said,

Women love only the man who will not
order them around when they are angry,
but, like a slave, mollify them:
the rest are just husbands: worthless.

The lovers best, both men and women,
are those who know the most superior
beds for pleasure. Of these there are
three types or categories.

The best, the least, the middling: there
are three types of lovers – man or woman;
their couches too are similarly
known to have divisions three.

Now, these are the qualities of gallants:

The lowest kind of lover
is a man who is scorched
by the flames of desire;
repeatedly scorned,
he remains infatuated
with the girl who disdains him.

The lover of the middling grade
is one whom passionate girls desire,
but he is too submissive, and
does not reciprocate.

But one whose love is constant
for a dear and devoted girl,
who longs for him intensely,
is the lover most excellent.

And of mistresses there are three kinds,

The one who is the best of all,
the moods of love does understand,
and is adept in acts of love;
she angers at the proper time, and
is quick to calm and please her man.

The lady of the middling kind
is proud and cringing by quick turns;
her anger, mostly out of place,
is hard, moreover, to placate.

The worst comes only out of greed,
she's fickle, speaks unpleasantly,
is expert in giving trouble
and lacking in all gratitude.

And of three types are the couples' beds

The best of lovers' couches
is higher on the sides
and sunken at the centre;
it will also bear the strong
poundings of a couple's passion.

> The middling bed is flat of surface,
> so that the night will often pass
> with rarely any contact
> between the bodies two.

> The worst is raised at the centre,
> and both its sides slope down;
> even adepts in the art cannot
> make love on it continuously.

It was on the best of beds that the learned Shubhankar made love to the queen. He let her go at daybreak, when she returned to the palace, fully satisfied.

As for the king, after completing his morning routine he sent for the poet and the queen. Seating Shubhankar on a throne, he talked to the poet and, in the course of conversation, said with a laugh: 'I believe that women only pretend they are afraid.'

On hearing these words the poet was amazed that his transgression was known to the king. The question is: what will happen now? There is punishment for trespass, even into the house of a poor man; how can it be avoided when the crime is committed against the king himself?

'The king knows about me,' the wise Shubhankar said to himself. Then he recited:

> Your mistress Fame, O mighty king,
> has crossed the cruel shark-filled sea;
> she roams the sky, without support,
> and mounts the crests of far-off hills;
> she goes alone to the nether world
> full of venemous serpent tribes;

O second Káma, I thus believe
that women only pretend they are afraid.

As he listened to the poet's recitation, the king gazed at him
and the queen. 'One so wise is hard to come by,' he said to
himself, 'but such women are not.' Then he grasped the queen's
hand and placed it in that of the learned poet, saying: 'Accept
this princess.'

'It is a great favour,' responded the delighted poet. It is
said,

How can one who has no learning
distinguish faults from merits?
Can one who is blind discern
blemishes in the human form?

By the king's grace the poet then lived happily with the lady
Chandralekha.

'If you too know what to say at the right time,' the parrot
concluded, 'then go, Prabhávati. Otherwise stay at home.' And
she retired to sleep after listening to this story.

Here ends the fifty-seventh tale of Shuka Saptati

58

Thε Plεdgε of a Kiss

A sked the next evening by Prabhávati who was ready to leave, the parrot said: 'Go for your tryst, eager one, if you know how to act as the occasion requires, as did Dusheela's husband before the god Ganapati.'

In the town of Lohapuri there lived a man of the plebian class named Rajad. His wife Dusheela, who was rather fond of men, would go with her friends to the city of Padmávati to sell yarn. Once all of them made separate vows before Ganapati at the god's temple located near a village. The passionate Dusheela pledged a kiss to the deity.

Ganapati enabled all the women to make large profits that day, and each one of them redeemed whatever she had pledged to the god. Dusheela took off all her clothes and gave Ganapati a kiss.

Ganapati loves dalliance. He caught hold of Dusheela's lip, so that she was stuck there like a chicken. Her friends reported this episode with much amusement to her husband in order to have her freed.

Rajad went to the temple and saw his wife in the condition which had been described to him. 'How can she be freed,' he wondered, and then started behaving passionately with a donkey. Ganapati laughed aloud at this curious sight, so that both his lips relaxed and Dusheela was released. Saluting the god, and scolding her husband, she promptly went home.

'My lady,' the parrot concluded, 'Rajad did what the occasion required, and freed Dusheela from Ganapati for his own benefit. The person who knows what to do acts according to the time and gains the fruit thereof. The man who understands the moment will always survive.'

After listening to this story Prabhávati retired to sleep.

Here ends the fifty-eighth tale of Shuka Saptati

59

Rukmini's Remarkable Deed

A t the end of the day Prabhávati asked the parrot as before
in order to go out. 'Go, lady,' said the bird, 'and do the
wonderful thing you have been thinking about, if you know
like Rukmini how to dupe a haughty husband.'

In the village of Sangam there lived a hot-tempered man of
the warrior caste named Ráhad. While going on a pilgrimage
with his wife Rukmini, he noticed that she and another man
were making eyes at each other, and concluded that she was
in love with him. It is said,

> He's the beau of that lovelorn maid,
> she's the girl with the looks so tender:
> in a village full of canny people
> even a breath is known to all.

Perceiving that his wife had been affected in this way, Ráhad
returned home and chained her inside after upbraiding her

harshly. As for Rukmini, she said to herself: 'My birth, life and youth will be fulfilled only if I lie with that other man before this one's very eyes.' Making up her mind, she promised this to herself; the question is, how will she carry out this pledge?

Seeing the other man pass by her home, she told him: 'Come tonight to my house and dig a trench the size of your body under the tamarind tree in the courtyard. Then you must lie down in the trench with your organ of manhood pointing upwards.

The man agreed and took his place at night accordingly. Then Rukmini, who was clever at doing everything as well as passionate, went under the shade of the tamarind and squatted upon the man. Calling out to her husband to come with his bow and arrow, she said to him: 'You are famous among the people as a great archer. Shoot me a moonbeam today so that I may see how great you are.'

The fool picked up his bow and arrow, took aim at a moonbeam, and released the shaft. Naturally, it could not pierce a ray of light in the sky, and fell to the ground after missing its target. At that she clapped her hands and mocked him, hereupon he went to look for his arrow and wandered about for a long time. Meanwhile she enjoyed herself in the reversed position with her lover. On her husband's return, she told him: 'You fool, today I have made love as I pleased before your eyes. You may be a warrior, but you are no good for me, and I am leaving you.'

Mounting a horse brought by her lover, she then went away, and Ráhad hid himself for shame on seeing her leave. Who can escape humiliation under the influence of women? For,

Shiva was made to dance a jig,
and so was Vishnu, in the past;
Brahma was treated like a beast;
who has not been vexed by women?

They are the root of this worldly round,
the ground which bears the sprouts of sin,
the bloom that has remorse as fruit,
what happiness do women bring?

This world is based on make-believe,
and that is caused by women;
with men, they need union, so,
eschew it and be at ease.

On hearing this, Prabhávati interjected,

Woman is the source of birth,
and she is the source of growth;
parrot, she is the source of pleasure,
how can you denigrate her?

Without her there cannot be
happiness or pleasure;
without her man will never find
fulfilment for himself.

'It is said,

A lake of nectar,
a mine of pleasure,
a treasure of love,
who made women thus?

Where is the need of anyone else
if you have seen the loved one?
Even the unhappiest mind
will be at peace with that sight.'

Having listened to Prabhávati's words, the parrot replied:

In metals, steeds and elephants,[1]
in woods and stones and garments,
in waters, men and women,
the differences are many.

'What you have said applies to chaste women, not to others.'

Prabhávati went to sleep after listening to this story.

Here ends the fifty-ninth tale of Shuka Saptati

60

The Marvellous Assembly Hall

The next day Prabhávati asked the parrot about her going out. 'Go, madam,' the bird replied, 'if you know what to do in case of doubt, as did the royal ambassador in King Vira's assembly hall.'

The ruler of Kaccha had heard that the king's assembly hall was most marvellous, that it had been constructed by a god and embellished with all kinds of jewels. To observe it he sent an ambassador named Hari Datta with many gifts including horses and gems of high quality.

After arrival in Vira's capital, the ambassador called on the king and said: 'I have been sent by my master to see your marvellous assembly hall.' 'I will show it to you in the morning,' the king replied.

On the following day the king sent for the ambassador, who suddenly found himself in the hall. He saw that it was studded with extraordinary jewels, but was unable to decide if it was built on land or on water. The question is: what should he do?

'He dropped a betel nut on the floor,' said the parrot, 'and discovered that it was land. After that he returned home.'

Prabhávati retired to sleep after listening to this story.

Here ends the sixtieth tale of Shuka Saptati

61

Tejuka and the Physician

Asked by her the next day, the parrot said: 'Go, my lady, if you know how to enjoy yourself with your lover, like Tejuka in times past. She did what she had long wanted to do.'

'What is this story?' Prabhávati asked, and this is the tale the parrot narrated.

In the village of Khorsam there was a man of the mercantile caste named Párshvanága, whose wife Tejuka was beautiful, passionate and unchaste. Once, while out with her woman friends to see a temple procession, she observed the looks of a handsome man and made up her mind to have him. For,

> A woman, madam, may be spoilt
> at wedding feasts and temple files,
> at palaces and strangers' homes,
> in disputes and in times of trouble.

It is said that this can happen at a house or a forest, a temple or a sacrificial ceremony, a ford or a lake, a wedding or a festival, and always in the premises of a female flower-seller. It happens during journeys and women's gatherings, in deserted places and in crowds, in towns and in villages, and specially to free and easy women who stand at their doors. It also happens in barns and fields, at mansions and crossroads, while travelling or living abroad and, during the arrivals and departures of kings, to women who always enjoy spectacles. Women unguarded by their husbands can lose their chastity in vacant neighbourhood houses; in the homes of laundresses and seamstresses; on royal highways; during daytime, night or evening; and in times of grief or trouble.

Tejuka signalled to the man with a movement of her eyebrows. 'I am in love with you,' she said to him, 'but my husband is harsh and intolerant, and I cannot dare to go out of doors. So, one of these days you should release a scorpion into the pot which is kept by the gate of our house. I will pretend to be stung by the scorpion, and you can come to our door as a physician.'

Both went home after this understanding. The man did as had been agreed, and Tejuka flung the pot at the bedstead, crying: 'I have been stung by the scorpion inside this pot.' This became her refrain.

The man pretended to be a physician and stood at the door. 'I can lance a boil, massage the stomach and relieve gripe,' he intoned, 'and I can extract venom.' Meanwhile Tejuka was telling her husband: 'Lord, there is no doubt that I will die!

Make my funeral pyre, or call doctors and exorcists to relieve me of this agony!'

The worried husband called in the man who stood outside the house. 'She has been stung by death itself,' this physician told him after looking at his wife. 'You will be lucky if she lives, and I shall become famous.'

'Be gracious, doctor,' the merchant entreated him, 'and free her from the poison.'

The physician then smeared Tejuka's lip with a bitter medicine. 'O merchant,' he told her husband, 'the strongest of all venoms is the venom of man. And poison is the remedy of poison. Bearing this in mind, you should suck her lip.'

The merchant commenced to act accordingly. But the taste of his wife's lip smeared with the medicine made his own mouth bitter within moments. 'You should suck the lip yourself,' he said to the other man, and stopped. Overcome with the suspicion of poison, he then went out, while his passionate wife was enjoyed by the sham physician at will.

The cunning Tejuka soon became well. The merchant too regained his calm. Full of gratitude, he fell at the physician's feet, saying 'I am in your debt for ever.' Thereafter, the other man would come to their house in the guise of a doctor, and always lie with Tejuka when the merchant was out.

'So, dear lady,' said the parrot, 'if you know how to act and speak like that, then go. Only a trickster, who knows how to speak and act similarly, should seek pleasure in this way.'

After listening to this story Prabhávati went to sleep.

Here ends the sixty-first tale of Shuka Saptati

62

The Two Wives of the Warrior

On the following day, when Prabhávati asked the parrot, the bird said: 'A lover should certainly be enjoyed, my lady. Go, as you desire that, but only if you can deal with an emergency like the two wives of Kuhan.'

In the village of Gambhir there lived a valiant but dull-witted man of the warrior caste named Kuhan. He loved women, but was also jealous and obstinate. He had two wives named Shobhika and Tejika, who were good looking, passionate, and promiscuous. For their protection he had built a house outside the village by the side of a river, and he would sit at its door to keep guard over them.

'It would be nice if a barber could come here,' the two wives once said to Kuhan, and he sent an itinerant one to them to pare their nails from behind a screen. As he began to wash their feet, which they had stretched outside the curtain, while the husband sat on the road nearby, they gave the barber

a bracelet of gold and told him secretly: 'Take this for money
and arrange a man for us.'

Having promised to do this, the barber took permission
from the warrior and went away. After some days he returned
with a young friend of his, whose beard was still to appear
but who knew what to do. The barber had dressed him like
a girl and, bringing him to the warrior, said: 'This is my
sweetheart. I wish to go to another village, and cannot leave
her anywhere except in Your Honour's house, where women
stay under due supervision.'

The warrior agreed, and the barber told his two wives:
'You both must make this one your very own.'

Shobhika and Tejika understood what the barber had
brought, and were very pleased. The youth would act the
woman all day, and turn lover at night, when he regularly
enjoyed both the spouses of the warrior.

Kuhan liked women, and himself wished to have a fling
with the new arrival. He would ask her for it every day, but
the make-believe maiden always declined. At last the warrior
began to wonder if she was a woman at all. To dispel his
suspicion he told his two wives: 'The goddess has ordained
that I should hold a festival in the morning. All three of you
will have to dance in the nude on that occasion.'

The question is: how will the one disguised as a woman
dance? The parrot gave the answer.

Pulling his genital back between his legs with a cord tied
to its tip, they created a clear representation of the female

organ on the young man. On the husband's arrival all of them clapped and danced, reciting:

> Behold the dancer who has gathered
> a web created in the mind;
> but ask not, for if it unravels,
> the man will take another wife.

Kuhan asked what was the meaning of the song. 'The girdle is called a web,' they said. 'If it breaks, the husband may take another wife. That is the meaning.' Ignorant of the ways of women, the warrior proved himself a fool; and the other man continued, in the garb of a girl, to enjoy his two wives as before.

'Thus, dear lady,' said the parrot, 'one who knows how to act and speak in an emergency, may go about in this world wherever he pleases, at his convenience and at any time.'

After listening to this story Prabhávati retired to sleep.

Here ends the sixty-second tale of Shuka Saptati

63

The Example of Shakatál

'I am going,' Prabhávati told the parrot next evening. 'Go, madam,' the bird replied, 'there is no harm in this if you know how to overcome any distress that you may have to suffer.'

'You too should be able to act like Shakatál, who overcame the distress caused in providing for his family by destroying the line of Nanda through Chanakya. If not, it is not proper for you to go to another man's house. It is said,

> Even the moon, lord of life-giving herbs,
> the stars his family, his body all nectar,
> loses his radiance in the solar orbit:
> who is not diminished in another's house?'

And Prabhávati went to sleep after listening to this story.

Here ends the sixty-third tale of Shuka Saptati

64

The Bull's Bell

On the following day Prabhávati again asked the parrot, who replied: 'O lady of the slender waist, go if you know how to do something in a crisis, like Devika did to save her friend's lover.'

'What is this story?' asked Prabhávati, and this is what the parrot narrated.

In the village of Kutapur there was a man of the warrior caste named Somraj, whose pretty wife Manduka was fond of other men. One of them would come at night with a bell as a sign, and sleep with her in the courtyard of the house.

Once the husband heard the chimes of the bell, and came running with a stick in his hand, thinking that a bull had come into the house. The question is: what will happen to that bull of a lover?

The parrot gave the answer. Seeing that Manduka's husband had come in response to the ringing of the bell, her friend

Devika sped the lover off and, taking the bell in her hand, told Somraj: 'Brother-in-law! The bull got frightened and ran away.' The warrior, on his part, went to his wife and told her what a wonderful thing he had done.

Prabhávati went away to sleep after listening to this story.

Here ends the sixty-fourth tale of Shuka Saptati

65

A Play of Words

Asked by Prabhávati the next day, the parrot said: 'It will be proper for you to go there, lady Prabhávati, if you know what to say in a crisis like the white-robed mendicant did when he was caught out.'

There is a town called Janasthan, my lady, which was ruled by the appropriately named king Nandan. In that town there lived a mendicant named Shrivatsa who was a great devotee of the god Shiva. Once, while on his way to Varanasi with his disciples, he sent one of them to get some meat. This was seen by the other mendicants, and the question is: what will happen now?

When all the mendicants had come and sat down, Shrivatsa burst out laughing. Asked by the others, he said: 'Look at this disciple! I said "turn towards me," and he turned towards the meat!'[1]

After listening to this story, Prabhávati went to sleep.

Here ends the sixty-fifth tale of Shuka Saptati

66

The Wise Swan

O n the following day Prabhávati asked the parrot as she was about to leave. 'Go, madam,' said the bird, 'good deeds should not be delayed if you know what to do in a time of danger like the wise king of the swans.'

There is in this land, madam, a beautiful forest dear to birds. It extends for ten yojanas, that is about eighty miles, and is almost free of human beings. After his daily wanderings, a king of the swans named Shankhadhavala would come there in the evening with his family to roost on a cool and shady banyan tree spreading by the side of a lake.

Once, while the swans were away on their rounds, a trapper spread his net on the tree, and they were caught in it when they returned at dusk. The question is: how can they save themselves? The parrot gave this answer.

Seeing that he and his family had been trapped that night, Shankhadhavala said: 'Children, when the trapper comes in the

morning, and climbs up the tree to look at you, remain still
without inhaling or exhaling, as if you are dead. Thinking that
to be the case, he will throw you down on the ground. Then
all of you should fly up and flee.'

The birds did as they were advised. The trapper came in
the morning and, thinking that they were dead, he threw them
down on the ground, whereupon they flew away to a place
of their choice.

Prabhávati retired to sleep after listening to this story.

Here ends the sixty-sixth tale of Shuka Saptati

67

The Monkey and the Crocodile

The next day Prabhávati once more asked the parrot as she was leaving. 'You are going because you are stricken by desire, gentle one,' said the bird. 'Go, then, if you know like the monkey what to say in your own interest.'

In the Pushpákara forest there lived a little monkey named Vanapriya. Once he saw a crocodile rolling about in the water on the sea shore. 'Friend,' he said, 'are you so fed up with life that you have come out on land today?'

'One's mind is content, monkey,' replied the crocodile, 'only in the place and in the livelihood ordained for one, and nowhere else. It is said,

> Lanka, filled with gold all over,
> O Lakshman does not please me;
> but Ayodhya, my patrimony,
> though poor, will give me joy.

One's mother and one's homeland,
life with a dear person,
love for wealth, a lovely woman,
and the last phase of sleep:
these are hard to give up.

'On seeing you, I feel that my life has been fulfilled. It is said,

To see good people is a blessing,
it is like a pilgrimage: visiting
shrines bears fruit in time,
but meeting the good
gives instant benefit.

'Blessed are those born on land,' the crocodile said in conclusion, 'where there are creatures with gentleness of speech like Your Honour.'

'O crocodile!' cried the monkey,. 'from today you are to me a friend dearer than my life. You speak with such affection. As has been said, even seven steps in the company of good people are sufficient to establish friendship.'

'Friend, be my guest today,' the monkey continued, and with these words he gave the crocodile a ripe fruit as sweet as nectar.

From that day the monkey would daily give bananas to the crocodile, who presented them to his wife. She asked her husband where they came from, and he told her all that happened.

The she-crocodile was pregnant. 'The monkey always eats such fruit,' she thought, 'his flesh must be like nectar.' Then she told her husband: 'Because of my pregnancy I have a craving to eat the flesh of a monkey's heart. If you satisfy this craving, I will live; otherwise there is no doubt that I will die.'

On the insistence of his wife, the crocodile came to the sea shore and told the monkey: 'Friend, your sister-in-law invites you to come and partake of hospitality in our house.' Convincing the ape with such words, he took him on his back and swam away. As he proceeded, the monkey became suspicious. 'What will I have to do at your place?' he asked.

'I have already brought this monkey away from the land,' the crocodile thought, 'How can he get back to the shore? So I will tell him all.' And he related the situation as it was. The question now is: what will happen to the monkey? The parrot continued the story.

'O crocodile, you are then taking me there for nothing,' said the monkey. 'For I am without a heart. My heart does not stay with me.'

'Where have you left it?' asked the crocodile.

'Have you not heard, friend?' the monkey replied. 'The hearts and minds of monkeys are always on fig or banyan trees. If you like, I can get it and come back into the water.'

The foolish crocodile returned to the seashore, and the ape jumped off his back and climbed up a tree. 'Go away,' he told the crocodile, 'now I am here and cannot be caught by such as you.

What the sages say is right:
the creatures who live and move
in water, and those of the land
can never go together.'

'Thus berated by the monkey,' the parrot said in conclusion, 'the crocodile returned to his home. It is said,

One who does not lose his wits
in works which need expedients:
he alone will find a haven
like the monkey in the sea.'

After listening to this story Prabhávati retired to sleep.

Here ends the sixty-seventh tale of Shuka Saptati

68

A Plea of Insanity

When Prabhávati spoke to the parrot on the following day, the bird said: 'My beauty, go and enjoy yourself if you have someone like Vitarka to aid you in a crisis.'

In a village of brahmins called Vidyasthana there lived a man of this priestly caste called Keshav. Once, when he had gone to the village lake for a bath, he saw the pretty daughter of a merchant filling vessels there, and wished to dally with her. As he came out after his bath, she asked him to place a pitcher of water on top of the one she had already positioned on her head. While doing this he kissed her on the lips.

The brahmin was seen in this act by the girl's husband, who took him to the royal court. The question is how will he save himself, and the parrot gave this answer.

The brahmin had a friend named Vitarka, who came and told him: 'Friend, when you get to the royal court, just mutter some gibberish, and say nothing else.' He followed this advice, after which the minister observed; 'This man is incoherent by nature. He cannot be held responsible for the transgression.'

'Thus was Keshav redeemed with the help of Vitarka's intelligence,' said the parrot. 'If you too can act similarly, then go.' But Prabhávati went to sleep after listening to this story.

Here ends the sixty-eighth tale of Shuka Saptati

69

How Vejika Saved Her Reputation

Asked by Prabhávati the next day, the parrot said: 'Take a lover, pretty eyes, if you can get away with it like Vejika did in the past with her half-bathed husband.'

In a place called Kalásthána there lived a man of the merchant caste with his wife Vejika, whom he loved dearly. Once she was giving her husband a bath when she observed her lover passing on the road as previously arranged. 'There is not enough water here,' she said, and going out of the house on the pretext of getting some more, she spent a long time with her paramour. The question is: what should she tell her husband who was abandoned halfway through his bath?

The parrot gave the answer. Having thought of a way to deceive her husband after being enjoyed by her lover, Vejika got herself down into a well. Then there was a commotion. The word spread that some poor woman had fallen into the well, and her husband also heard about it. 'It must certainly be my wife who has fallen into the well,' he worried, and quickly went to investigate. He then pulled her out and took her home with all consideration.

Prabhávati went to sleep after listening to this story.

Here ends the sixty-ninth tale of Shuka Saptati

70

The Final Story

At the conclusion of these stories, Prabhávati's husband
Madan returned from abroad. On his arrival she became
as loving towards him as she had been before, while the parrot
recited softly:

> Attachment to women is futile,
> and futile too is the conceit
> that 'she will always love me,
> and will be my beloved for ever.'

As Madan did not pay any attention to this stanza, the parrot
laughed and said: 'One who heeds the words said for his benefit,
and acts upon them, earns merit both in this and the next world.'
The bird repeated this again and again, till Madan listened and
asked what this was about. At this point a worried Prabhávati
herself began to explain. It is said,

Proud of the power of their good deeds,
righteous men are free of fear;
but, worried by their evil acts,
the sinful are always scared.

'Noble one,' said Prabhávati to her husband, 'you deserve praise for having in your house this parrot, which is one of the pair brought here by Trivikram. This bird gives good advice to everyone, and to me specially, has been like a father or brother.'

The more she praised the parrot, the more the bird looked abashed. It is said,

If the crane catches fish,
it earns him no respect;
but honoured is the lion
who slays the mighty elephant.

'How has this parrot acquired such merits?' asked Madan. 'Has it done you some special service?'

'Master,' Prabhávati replied, 'there are few speakers or listeners for words of truth. It is said,

It is always easy to find
people who speak sweetly, O King;
of that which is wholesome but bitter,
both speaker and listener are rare.

Woman is fickle, O master,
devoid of merit or love,
suspicious too, and small minded:
this has been truly said.

She turns away from son and husband,
considers not great favours done;
loving and tender at the start,
she's cruel when it suits her.

'It is said,

They are kind as long as men
do not fall in love with them;
once they know them to be caught
in Káma's noose, they will then play
with them as with a fish
which has swallowed the bait.

Their moods keep passing,[1]
like waves upon the sea;
their love lasts a moment,
like light on clouds at dusk;
their purpose served,
they will discard
the man without money
like seeds squeezed dry.

> Entering the kindly heart of man,[2]
> what cannot a damsel do:
> enchant, drive mad, humiliate,
> berate, give joy and sorrow too?

'Master,' Prabhávati continued, 'when you went away, for some time I could bear being separated from you. But then I fell into bad company, and wanted to take a lover. I nearly killed the mynah which tried to stop me, but then this parrot held me back for seventy days with his flow of words. Thus I sinned only in thought, but never by deed. Now my life and death are in your hands.'

After listening to his wife Madan asked the parrot, and the bird said:

> The wise man will not speak about
> anything without knowing its purpose;
> and, even knowing it, will not
> speak in haste; for the turns of fate
> can never be anticipated.

'It was fated that, after a long time, you should be restored to your possessions and to your life with your beloved. All that she said is correct. It was entirely a situation which arose from being alone.'

'Listen to this master,' the parrot continued, 'even though it may not be proper to say it,

Noble people are forgiving,
and ignore both bad and good
deeds of fools and drunkards,
of women, the sick and the dejected,
those driven by anger or lust,
the mad, the scared and, specially,
those who are desperate with hunger.

'It is said in the *Mahabharata*,

Know, Dhritaráshtra, that these ten
do not dharma understand:
the mad, the heedless and the drunk,
the tired, angry and the starving,
the greedy, frightened and the lustful,
and those who are in a hurry.

'Her misdeed should be forgiven, for it was not her fault but
due to the company of wicked friends. It is said,

The good are affected by keeping
company with the wicked;
associating with Duryodhan,
Bhishma went stealing cows.

'A vidyádhara or demigod once seduced a king's daughter by
a trick,' the parrot added. 'But even though she was well and
truly seduced, her husband considered her to be innocent.'
The bird then related a story to Madan.

On the crest of Mount Malaya there is a city of the gandharvas or a class of celestial beings called Manohara. A gandharva named Madan lived there with his wife Ratnávali. Their daughter Madan Manjari was so beautiful that everyone, god or demon, would bow his head, for fear of enchantment, on seeing her. But there was no one worthy enough to whom she could be given in marriage.

Once the divine sage Nárada came to Manohara, and was so aroused on beholding the beauty of Madan Manjari that he fainted. On regaining his senses, the sage cursed her, and said:

> This lovely girl, more sweet than love,
> handsome, always full of passion,
> a source of joy, if such a beauty,
> steals my heart, can I ever win?

'As I was stricken with Káma's fever on seeing her beauty,' the sage declared, 'she will one day lose her chastity.'

The gandharva king fell at the sage's feet. 'May it please you,' he said, 'be gracious, master.'

'She will not be faulted for the loss of her chastity,' said the sage, 'nor will it cause any alienation from her husband. There is a gandharva named Kanakaprabha who lives in the city of Vipula on Mount Meru. He will be your daughter's husband.' And, with these words, the sage departed.

In keeping with the sage's pronouncement, Madan Manjari was married to Kanakaprabha. Once he went to Mount Kailasa, leaving her behind. Distraught at being separated from him, she was reclining on a rock without her clothes and other adornments when her remarkable beauty was observed by a certain vidyádhara, who invited her to lie with him. She declined, but he assumed the form of her husband and seduced her.

In due course Madan Manjari's husband returned home and found her in that state of contentment which comes after the pleasures of sexual intercourse. 'Someone else has enjoyed her body,' he said to himself on seeing her, and decided that she deserved to die. He took her to the temple of the goddess Chandika, and was about to slay her before the deity, when Madan Manjari cried out: 'Mistress! You have given me the boon that my son will become the paramount king of the gandharvas. How can I die without seeing his face?'

As Madan Manjari lamented in this manner, the goddess addressed her husband: 'O brave gandharva, your wife is not at all at fault. A vidyádhara assumed your appearance by magic and seduced her. She was unaware of this and cannot be blamed for it. Moreover there was also the curse of the sage upon her.'

The goddess recounted the story of the sage's curse. 'In accordance with his words, she is innocent,' the goddess said, 'and you should accept her.' The gandharva's doubts were set at rest after listening to the divine Gauri,[3] and he took his wife home, where they lived happily.

'Therefore, merchant's son,' said the parrot, 'if you believe me, you should be gracious to this innocent lady.' And Madan accepted her on the parrot's urging.

Happy at his son's return, Hari Datta held a great festival during which a celestial garland came down from heaven. On seeing it the parrot, the mynah, and the brahmin Trivikram were freed from their curse and ascended to paradise. And Madan lived happily on earth with his beloved Prabhávati.

Here ends the seventieth tale of Shuka Saptati

Notes

Introduction

1. M. Winternitz, *History of Indian Literature*, Calcutta 1927. Tr. Subhadra Jha, Delhi 1985.
2. A.B. Keith, *A History of Sanskrit Literature*, London 1920.
3. S.N. Dasgupta, ed., *A History of Sanskrit Literature*, vol. I, Calcutta 1947.
4. M. Krishnamachariar, *History of Classical Sanskrit Literature*, 1937.
5. L. Sternbach, *The Kávya Portions in the Kathá Literature*, Delhi 1976.
6. Saroja Bhate, in *Glimpses of Sanskrit Literature*, ed. A.N.D. Haksar, New Delhi 1995.
7. Cf. 1 above.
8. A.K. Warder, *Indian Kávya Literature*, vol. 6, New Delhi 1992.
9. Cf. 5 above.
10. Ibid. Except for its concluding sentence, this section is based mainly on Sternbach, whose work contains the last detailed account of research on the *Shuka Saptati*, and translations of the work.

11. Ibid. Benfey, quoted by Sternbach.
12. V. Raghavan, quoted by Warder, cf. 8 above.

Prologue

1. Another name of Sarasvati, the goddess of learning in the Hindu pantheon.
2. Literally, the righteous hunter. The story of the Dharma Vyadha occurs in the *Mahabharata*, III 207-19, and is retold here in summary form.

Tales of the Parrot

Tale 1

1. Three legendary examples of burdens borne for the greater good. The god Shiva consumed the poison which would have otherwise destroyed the world. The god Vishnu, in his incarnation as Kúrma or tortoise, sustained the earth upon his back. The Ocean contains a great fire. Sternbach traced this verse to the earlier works, *Chanakyaniti* and *Chaurapanchaśika*. The sourcing of other verses in these notes is also from Sternbach, cf. Introduction note 5.

Tale 2

1. Also found in *Chanakyaniti*.

Tale 5

1. This well-known verse also occurs in the *Mahabharata*, the *Chanakyaniti* and the *Hitopadeśa*.
2. Also found in the *Hitopadeśa*, 2.58.

Tale 6

1. Legendary instances of irrational actions by otherwise sensible people, leading to disaster. The stories of Rama being lured by a demon disguised as a golden deer, and of Yudhishthira gambling away his wife and brothers are well-known from the epics. King Nahush used holy sages as beasts of burden, and was cursed by them to lose his throne. King Kartavirya Arjuna stole the sage Jamadagni's cattle, and was slain by his son, the divine incarnation Parashurama.

Tale 7

1. The god of love and desire. The word also refers to these emotions and occurs repeatedly in this work.

Tale 8

1. A class of demigods. Their cults seem to have been current, specially in rural areas, and they are mentioned repeatedly in these stories.

Tale 9

1. Also in *Chanakyaniti*, 7.1.

Tale 10

1. The plant barleria cristata. Jhinti in Sanskrit.

Tale 11

1. This verse also occurs in tale 1.
2. According to one legend, Rukmini had been betrothed to Shishupala, a cousin of Krishna, when she fell in love with the latter and eloped with him.

3. A group of sages. The legend occurs in the *Shiva Purana*.

Tale 15

1. See tale 8, note 1.
2. The European Indologist M. Winternitz considered that this story was the prototype of Gottfried von Strassburg's *Tristan and Isolde*. See the introduction.

Tale 17

1. Also found in the *Markandeya Purana* and the *Parashara Dharma Samhita*.
2. This verse also occurs in tale 9.

Tale 19

1. See tale 8, note 1.
2. Also found in the *Hitopadeśa*, 1.195.

Tale 20

1. The modern Sabarmati in Gujarat.

Tale 21

1. This and the immediately following verse are also found in the *Panchatantra*.
2. It was believed that some hunters mesmerised deer with music in order to catch them.
3. The epic poem *Kirátarjuniya* of Bharavi.

Tale 23

1. This verse is from the *Kumárasambhava* of Kalidasa, 7.22.

2 This popular verse also occurs in the *Mahabarata* and the *Hitopadeśa*.

Tale 26

1. From the *Kirátarjuniya* of Bharavi.

Tale 30

1. A famous trickster in Sanskrit literature, who reputedly authored a manual on thieving.

Tale 32

1. Some scholars think that this Sanskrit name for a coin derives from the Greek drachma. Also used in tale 45.

Tale 39

1. Similar language is also used in tale 6. The idea is that one's good and bad deeds in previous lives provide a balance of merit which determines one's wellbeing in the present life. Hence the need for continued good deeds to keep the balance replenished.

Tale 41

1. In token of accepting the offer or challenge under proclamation. This action also occurs in tales 21 and 46.
2. The original verses are in Prakrit from which they were rendered into Sanskrit. In the absence of English equivalents, some plant names are given in the original.

Tale 45

1. See tale 32, note 1.

Tale 48

1. This verse is from the play *Mudrárákshasa* of Viśákhadatta.
2. Also in Ballala's *Bhojaprabandha*, 15.

Tale 51

1. The three pursuits of virtue (dharma), material gain (artha), and pleasure (káma) were regarded as the objectives of worldly life. The fourth, salvation (moksha), was a spiritual pursuit.

Tale 56

1. See tale 8, note 1.

Tale 59

1. Also found in the *Garuda Purana*, 110.

Tale 65

1. The tale turns on a pun in Sanskrit, which can give both meanings.

Tale 70

1. This verse is from Sudraka's play, *Mricchakatika*, 4.15.
2. This verse is also found in Bhartrhari's *Satakatrayi*, 326, and Krishna Mishra's *Prabodha Chandrodaya*, 1.27.
3. Another name of the same goddess.